DATE DUE

Hatfield			
M 01			
Dockery			
Owens			
E.97.69			
W&F 1-13-06			
Sears			
BL			
VAUGHT 07			
R. Simpson			
W. Jenkins			
Aug 08			
GAYLORD			PRINTED IN U.S.A.

Trail of
the Sioux

OTHER SAGEBRUSH LARGE PRINT WESTERNS BY
LAURAN PAINE

Buckskin Buccaneer
Bags and Saddles
Guns of the Law
Six Gun Atonement
The Californios
The Catch Colt
The Guns of Summer
The Past Won't End
The Rawhiders
The Sheridan Stage
Valor in the Land

Trail of
the Sioux

LAURAN PAINE

Sagebrush
Large Print Westerns

Library of Congress Cataloging-in-Publication Data

Paine, Lauran.
    Trail of the Sioux / Lauran Paine'
        p.   cm.
    ISBN 1-57490-345-4 (alk. paper)
    1. Northwestern States—Fiction. 2. Dakota Indians—Fiction.
3. Large type books. I. Title.

PS3566.A34 T74 2001
813'.54—dc21   2001019046

    Cataloging in Publication Data is available from the British
Library and the National Library of Australia.

Sagebrush Large Print Westerns are published in the United
States and Canada by Thomas T. Beeler, Publisher, PO Box 659,
Hampton Falls, New Hampshire 03844-0659. ISBN 1-57490-345-4

Published in the United Kingdom, Eire, and the Republic of
South Africa by Isis Publishing Ltd, 7 Centremead, Osney
Mead, Oxford OX2 0ES England. ISBN 0-7531-6442-6

Published in Australia and New Zealand by Bolinda Publishing
Pty Ltd, 17 Mohr Street, Tullamarine, Victoria, Australia, 3043
ISBN 1-74030-299-0

Manufactured by Sheridan Books in Chelsea, Michigan.

CHAPTER I

"ORDINARILY," JACOB HARTER SAID, "WE'D KEEP THE freighters to the flat country where the going is easier, but the Indians are bad now, so we sort of skip and hop from ridge to ridge. We can see around more, and it gives us places to hide or fort up, if we have to."

The girl riding beside him was slim, straight, handsome, with a strong face, sky-blue eyes, and a composed, wide mouth. She gazed over the immensity. There was nothing moving anywhere. Miles and miles of nothing. Trees along the ridges here and there, rich, green grass turning dun-brown, a brass-yellow sun in a faded sky frayed a little at the outer extremities. It was Northwest Territory—Indian country.

Harter's chestnut beard had fiery lights in it that even the trail dust couldn't subdue. His position in the saddle was erect; still almost, and uncomfortably alert. While his head swung like a wolf's from side to side with never-ending vigilance, his mind considered once more the circumstances that had given this girl's care into his hands. He wasn't pleased about it at all.

Her father had the buggy works at Clybourne, a rag-tag village that had come into being out of the necessity, and the desire, of people to huddle together in the face of Indian trouble. The town had grown and prospered, sustained mostly by the fear that trouble would come again. It had. Caleb Mellon's Buggy Works. Harter's shifting eyes grew ironic. Fancy name for a glorified blacksmith shop. Still, Mellon was a good wagon maker. Who should know better than the freighters whose rigs needed constant repair and care?

1

Old Mellon had sent her to visit his kinsmen in the 'States when Red Cloud and the others went wild, two years back. Harter nodded his head over that. It had been wisely done, but why in the name of all that was holy did the tomfool fetch her back now?

What had happened two years before had been child's play alongside what was happening now. He thought of things he'd seen himself, and of other things he knew. Then he let his gaze rest briefly, pityingly, on the girl. Jacob Harter was too old to curl his handsome beard for her, but he still worried about her.

The brace of years had changed the girl, too. She was a willowy woman now where she'd been a lanky girl before. Pretty? Yes, but that didn't describe her exactly—not fully. She had a strength, an erectness to her carriage, a litheness that came from health and poise and something else. It might be courage, although he didn't know. Assessing the merits of mules and horses was more in his line.

"Elizabeth, don't the papers back East carry the news about what's going on out here?"

She swung her head until the blue eyes rested fully on his bearded face. "Yes," she said thoughtfully, "but the news they print is usually several months old. It's distorted too, Mr. Harter. There are only two kinds of newspapers back East. One says we're murdering helpless savages. The others say we aren't killing enough of them fast enough. People don't know what to think. Some of the folks I met practically said all of us out here were no better than the savages, and the others seemed to think we were all insane to live out here."

"Well," Harter said flintily, "there's a mite of truth in that, Elizabeth. Take freighting. What's the good of the money you make taking long chances if you don't live to spend it?"

2

She smiled, thinking he had been a handsome man twenty years before. He was still good-looking, but in a forbidding way. "You'll live to spend your money. Anyone who is as vigilant as you are will come through all right."

His mouth beneath the beard parted and drew downward in a knowing grimace. "Elizabeth, I'm going to tell you something. It doesn't matter how vigilant a man is; the odds're against him." He twisted in the saddle and flung out a thick arm, pointing backwards and downwards. "See there? See those tracks? That's our Last Mile any time a bronco buck stumbles across it. Vigilance be hanged. Look up there at those wagons. Big, aren't they? Bigger'n any wagons ought to be. That's so's they can haul a heavy pay-load. Well, you sacrifice speed for strength with big wagons, Elizabeth." He stopped there and looked at her. "You see? Understand what I'm getting at?" Without waiting for her nod, he went on. "The Sioux and Cheyennes travel fast. They can ride rings around the wagons any day of the week. The tracks we cut into the land lead them to us. We can't run, Elizabeth, and if they're even halfway on the prod and anywhere near our numbers, we're in a bad spot." He put both hands on the saddlehorn and began his restless sweep of the country around them again. Contented with having said just that much, his jaws clamped tightly shut.

She let the silence linger, not caring to pursue the conversation, since her own fears were deep and solid, like the fears of every man in the party. Instead she looked at the landscape, remembering it, feeling a nostalgic oneness with it.

Northward was the pure sweep of plains broken by little land-swells and ridges. Far off was the blue-purple

3

majesty of the great bony mountains, huge and craggy and awesome. Closer was the blur of heat-haze, the smell of curing grass, the buffalo wallows, the creeks and willow-furze, the shimmering rocks here and there, and the eternal hush—the ominous silence.

Closer still was the grunt and creak of the chain-harnesses and the sounds of giant wheels turning, grinding, furrowing the ground with their wide iron tires. Occasionally there were flies, too, drawn by the reeking sweat-smell of the mules and horses, and other odors just as strong of men and animals toiling under a scathing sun.

Harter jolted her out of her reverie when he said: "Here comes Jess. I hope it isn't trouble."

She watching the lean man jogging back from the far point of the train on his big chestnut horse. Curiosity piqued her. Before he got close she asked Harter about him. The freight-master shrugged, watching the rider approaching.

"You know how it is, Elizabeth. They come and they go. He's a top scout. Not much of a freighter. Name's Jess Swindin. I never asked where he came from but I got a hunch he's been out here a spell. Handles himself like an old hand. I know he knows Indians. One time on Hat Creek we fell in with a bunch of Shoshones. He held a regular powwow with them by hand-talk—sign language. Indians call it *wibluta*."

Swindin was too close now. Harter fell silent, and Elizabeth studied the tall man on the big horse. Beneath perfectly straight brows was the direct, appraising line of grey eyes. He had a strong mouth and a jaw that was relaxed. She guessed he could chill a man to the bone or winnow out the blackness from a wild horse's heart. The structure of his face was strong and pleasant, with

4

definite, hard contours. His dress was the nondescript, comfortable attire of all frontiersmen, part Indian, part white. He wore high-topped cowhide boots with low flat heels. Into these were stuffed woollen pants of shapeless make and uncertain vintage. His shirt was butternut-grey, and over it he wore a smoke-tanned coat with bone buttons and geometric designs in beadwork. The coat was Indian. So was the sheath that held his belt-knife. The drover's hat he wore low, to protect his eyes, was stiff-brimmed and flat-crowned. It was designed and worn for strictly utilitarian purposes, like the walnut-butted Dragoon revolver with the long barrel that slapped rhythmically at his lean thigh.

She had seen him before, and he her, but neither had so much as nodded to the other up to now. That was what aroused her curiosity. He had avoided her. Now, though, he couldn't. They both knew it when he reined up, turned, waited for Jacob Harter to ride in beside him, and threw Elizabeth a slow nod.

He didn't smile. For a second she thought his face looked as though he had forgotten how to smile, it was so solemn and impassive. But his eyes were different. In their directness she caught a hint of something, as though he were looking at her objectively, measuring her beside some image of women he had known. It disturbed her and she looked away. Then he spoke.

"Bucks east of us, Jake. Three on a ridge. Too far to make out who they are, but it doesn't matter. We're in sight of Clybourne."

"Can they get between us?" Jacob asked with a quick frown.

"No, they're too far off. Anyway, I'd guess them to be part of a hunting party. No feathers and foofaraw."

Harter nodded and smothered a mild curse, lifted his

5

glance and threw it ahead where the heat-haze looked a little darker and cloudier. He should've felt relief but he didn't. Instead he felt worried. "Gossip said they wouldn't be down here yet. Too early."

Jess Swindin looked sardonically in the direction he'd seen the Indians. His words were made softer by his face being averted. "I wouldn't say that, Jake. In the spring they come out of hibernation like a bear, starved and restless, looking for the first coup of the year. They need new horses to replace the ones that've starved to death during the winter. They need meat and a scalp or two. No, I wouldn't say they'd put off coming down to the white-man settlements a day longer than they have to."

He turned then and gazed at Jacob. Just beyond the bearded face was Elizabeth. He was instantly conscious of her steady look and concentrated on the wagon master, refusing to be drawn away by her regard. "We'll make it all right anyway," he said, and lifted his reins preparatory to riding away.

"I wasn't thinking about this trip, Jess. I was thinking about the next one," Harter said.

Jess said nothing, but he lowered his rein hand to the saddlehorn, waiting.

Harter looked at neither of them. Balefully, he regarded his cumbersome, mighty freighters, each with a driver and a swamper high on the exposed seat. "We've got nine loads of Army goods to take up-country after we unload this stuff."

Softly Jess asked, "How soon?"

Harter's troubled, pensive gaze swung and fastened itself to the scout's face. "As soon as we unload. This has been waiting for us to get back. It's plenty urgent, according to what I hear. In order to make it to Fort

Ten-Mile fast, we have to leave Clybourne no later'n day after tomorrow."

Swindin's eyes flickered to Elizabeth's face for a fraction of a second, then swung in a roving arc back out over the countryside. He said nothing.

Elizabeth saw his big-knuckled hands tighten on the reins. He looked so totally relaxed and composed all the time, so unruffled and calm and equal to anything, that the gesture was frightening.

She knew Ten-Mile. The Army had thrown it up on a little ledge overlooking the immigrant trail six years before. It was a stodgy, crude place made of rammed earth, logs, fear and sweat. It had been attacked so many times by the Sioux and Northern Cheyennes there was hardly a foot of outer wall and palisade that didn't have bullet pocks in it. Arrow shafts were sawed off flush with the wall almost as methodically as the watch was changed every few hours within the fort. It had been given its name because the ten-mile stretch of country between Clybourne and the fort was known the breadth of the northwestern country as the most harrowing, most deadly stretch of road the white men controlled.

She also knew that their huge wagons, loaded, didn't make better than ten miles a day. Their snail's pace had galled her all the way from the Missouri, where a steamer had landed her for the last leg of her journey from the 'States.

Jess lifted his left hand again, threw Elizabeth that same strange, appraising look, then ignored her in favor of Jacob Harter. "Well," he said, "we'll have two days' grace at Clybourne." Then he rode ahead in a long lope. Harter hadn't replied. Elizabeth watched Jess go, thinking that in this land where all men, red and white, rode well, Jess Swindin rode better. It might be because

7

of his leanness or his long legs. She thought it was more likely because of something her father had said repeatedly: "Some men just belong on horses and nowhere else." He rode like one who did.

"There's Clybourne," Harter said.

She peered beyond the farthest freighter, wallowing its way down a gentle incline toward the level country ahead, and saw the town. The heat made it quiver but it looked almost the same. There were a few more shacks on the outskirts, a little more dust above it, but mainly it remained as she remembered it. The dusty roads turned to quagmires in the winter. Bleached, warped siding with the sap still running from it was on the buildings. The whole town leaned into itself as though seeking protection against the blizzards of winter, the curling heat of summer, and the fierce antagonism of the Indians in whose land it squatted.

"It's been a long trip." Until she said it she had no idea how tired and distraught she was.

Harter turned and saw her slump a little in the saddle. There were tiny beads of perspiration on her upper lip and a rich red flush high on her face under each eye. For a freighter and a blunt man, he made a gallant remark: "You're the only thing I ever saw sweating that looked pretty, Elizabeth."

She was startled but she smiled at him. Back East his remark would have been greeted with cold silence. This wasn't the same country at all. Oh, the flag was the same, but nothing else was. Neither the country, the people, or the manners. "It'll be pleasant to sit in the shade for a change."

He nodded, still sober-faced. "It will for a fact."

She watched his profile and thought, if ever a man had blind stubbornness and courage etched in his

8

features—blasted there by life in a savage land—Jacob Harter had. What she said was: "Has Clybourne changed much?"

"About like you'd expect, Elizabeth," he said, watching the town come up to them. "The Indian wars've brought a lot more people in from the country. More shacks, more dogs, more dirty little kids in the alleys is about all. Soldiers, too, coming and going. Scouts—tame Indians." He glanced at her.

"Your paw's business has about trebled. He keeps the forges going day and night. Mostly he's up to his shoulders in overhauling and repairing. Not much call for new vehicles any more. He's making a new kind of wagon though. Made especially for this country. It's a good one."

Then the noises of Clybourne came to her, and from them she knew what her home town would be like. Everything was bustle and excitement. Even the traffic, when the huge freighters swung wide to go around the town where Jacob Harter's corrals were, was heavier than she'd dreamed it would be. Dogs were everywhere. People seemed turned out as though for some kind of a celebration. She knew they weren't though; they were just the swollen population of the village.

The last night she said to Jacob Harter, before she left word to have her luggage sent to her father's house, was: "It really must be bad, Mr. Harter. I didn't think of it as being so close until we got into town."

Jacob's eyebrows went up. He studied her for a moment in silence; then he said: "Elizabeth, it's plenty bad. It's a real war this time, not just a few bronco bucks out to lift hair and steal horses. It's a real war and it's along way from over." Then he swung down beside her, looking more massive-chested than he did on a

9

horse, and added, "Reading about it in a newspaper back East sort of makes it seem a long way off, I know, but you're smack-dab in the middle of it now, and no mistake. Don't let anyone tell you different, Elizabeth, and don't forget for a minute you're not back East any more."

He nodded to her and walked away. She reined her horse out into the roadway's traffic, puzzling over his last remark.

Her father's house was solid and permanent. It had a tasselated curtain of long glass beads cut in a gentle curve, between the parlor and the dining room, and its furniture was the kind that freighters hated and envied when they had to risk their lives to haul it from Independence. The place, since her mother's death four years before, had come to look more and more like a bachelor's home. The smell of cigar smoke was always in the air, but it was home and she loved it. As she stood in the hallway, a flood of memories overwhelmed her for a moment. She stood still, fighting down the unshed tears that burned behind her eyes. Then her father was there, his big face glistening from the warmth, wearing a breathless sort of expression, eyes shining.

"Honey, by God you're a lady." He said it all at once without a pause between the words.

Then she was swept into his arms and the tears came. She could feel him stiffen and picture the bewilderment on his face and burrowed deeper against him, smelling the cigar smoke stronger than ever.

"What's the matter, honey? Tired? Worn out?" He tried to back away gently, but she held onto him until he stood still and let her cry it out; then she pinched his big arm and looked up at him.

"I'm tired, I guess."

"Well, I had your room slicked up. You go get some rest and I'll be home for supper." He held her at arm's length and gazed at her. There was something akin to awe in his eyes. "You're a picture, Liz," he said. "You're just like your mother was at twenty. I didn't know a couple of years'd do that to you." He let his arms drop. "A grown lady. A real grown-up lady, Liz."

She dabbed at her face, felt its flushed warmth and smiled up at him. "You're the handsomest man I've seen since I left the river—but if you made those infernally slow wagons you ought to be switched. Ten miles a day! Oh! I thought we'd never get here."

He smiled again, the awe gone and his customary good nature restored in all its bluster and strength. "I'll get home early tonight and we'll talk wagons." He started toward the door, then said, "I'm powerful glad you're home, Liz. I missed you, girl."

"Go on," she said swiftly, feeling the tears returning. "I'll be home a long time. We've got years to talk."

He nodded and left the house. When she was alone, the memories instantly crowded back. She hurried to her room and cleaned up. The sounds of Clybourne rode the summer air like banners, each in a different key. An hour later, fresh and rested, she was going back into the parlor when a heavy hand thumped the door. It was Harter's scout, Jess Swindin. She was surprised to see him carrying her cowhide portmanteau and her little carpetbag. Without a word he set them both down. When he straightened up she saw his face. It was embarrassed-looking. Their glances met. Before she could speak, he said, "The swamper who was supposed to bring the things hurt his ankle."

"I'm sorry. If I'd known I'd have sent someone down. You were very kind to do this."

11

He startled her then. With a slow look he gazed at the dress she'd put on in place of her billowing riding clothes. Almost wistfully he said: "That's a very pretty dress. Is that what they're wearing in the 'States now?"

There was something painful behind his words. She felt it. "No, this is an old one, one I had here before I left." She felt her color heightening, for while she had been putting the dress on she'd been been conscious that it was tighter on her than it had been two years before.

He raised his eyes to her face. The directness of his glance, grave and steady, added to her confusion. "You are very pretty in it."

It angered her that she couldn't think of a solitary word to say. Her tongue was like a piece of wood. It was ridiculous.

"Well—goodbye."

She nodded stiffly and watched him stride down the path to the boardwalk, turn south toward Harter's corrals and thread his way among the passersby. Then her embarrassment and confusion dropped away and only her vexed feeling remained. She closed the door and stared at her luggage, swung past it, hesitated, went back and rummaged for a dress she was especially fond of—the latest thing, really—and went into her bedroom.

By early evening her father came home. When she stood up he gazed at her with the same awed expression he'd worn earlier, and said solemnly, "Liz, it just doesn't seem that a girl can turn into a woman in so short a time."

"Two years is a long time, Dad."

His eyes crinkled. "Is it?" he said mockingly. "Then I am older'n the hills."

They ate and talked. Her father drained her of news of their relations back in the 'States, absorbed all she told him with the patient, mannerly look of a person who has just completed a particularly colorless task; then he launched into the one topic that was foremost in his own world—wagons.

"Business is booming, Liz. But I'm having trouble sandwiching the wagons I want to make between the Army Quartermaster repairs and the usual freighter overhauls."

"Why try, Dad?"

"Why?" he said briskly, in a tone of voice that showed he'd thought this out many times. "Because when this Indian trouble's over, honey, there'll be more demand than ever before for a stout, light spring-wagon. Every immigrant and every settler and every peddler'll need one; a light wagon built for this country, strong as iron but light enough for one team to pull."

She knew how he loved buggies. She had seen many he'd made by hand with low, sweeping lines, frail wheels and raciness. "What about your buggies?"

He chuckled, guessing her thoughts. "Liz, I've learnt something these past few years. Sure, I want to make buggies. I'd rather make buggies than anything—you know that. Well, I've learnt that I've got to give the settlers a good work wagon first; then they'll be able to make their ranches and farms pay enough so they can come back and buy my buggies."

She watched his expression alter while he talked of thorobracing, couplings, running-gear—all the intimate craftsman's terms of his business.

"What about the Indians, Dad?"

His face changed abruptly. His eyes clouded and his bulk settled deeper into the chair. His cigar drooped so that the smoke drifted up into his face, making him squint his blue eyes, and lent him a solemn, unfriendly look.

13

"The Indians." He said it like a pronouncement. "Liz, you've been away. Right up until a couple of years ago we had scares every week or so. Those were raiding parties, young bucks out to steal horses—so forth. Well, that's all changed. Now it's a regular confederacy of the Dakotas—folks call them Sioux, and the Northern Cheyennes. It isn't just the individual bands, it's the whole bunch of them—every band of both tribes. Dog Soldiers—the whole kaboodle."

She listened to him talk and thought back to the nights she'd slept in one of Jacob Harter's huge freight wagons, hearing the sleep-drowsy talk of the men. Out there names and places had been mentioned. Her father spoke now of the same names and places. Lame Deer, Crazy Horse, General Miles, Iron Star, Red Cloud, Colonel Custer, General Terry, American Horse, Battle of Washita, old Black Kettle, Beecher's Island, Lodgepole Pines . . . Names and places and terrible massacres retold. Murders, tortures, horror. The East was far, far away. That had been what Jacob Harter had meant. She understood. This was an altogether different world.

She stirred in her chair, and her father's eyes came down from unblinking regard of the wall just above her head. He forced a smile and said, "This is no way to talk your first night home. We don't have to bring this stuff to supper with us. It's all folks talk about all day long, anyway. Let's talk about you."

"One more question, Dad. Folks back East used to show me the papers and ask if it was true what they read: that the Indians numbered well up in the thousands."

"What did you tell them?"

"I told them I'd never seen more than twenty to fifty in one band."

"Well," Caleb Mellon said slowly, "that was a couple

14

of years back, Liz. Now they're in no more than a half-dozen big villages. Maybe somewhere between two to five thousand to a village."

She was astounded. "I didn't think they numbered that many all together."

"A lot of folks didn't. I was one of them." He waved a big arm toward the western wall of the room. "We don't know their country, Liz. What the old trappers told us we laughed at. Now it looks like there are ten thousand or so of them." He let his arm drop. "That wouldn't be too many if the government'd send soldiers, but all we get is dribbles—handfuls now and then." He shrugged apathetically. "All right, they have to police the South, but the thing is—we've got a war out here. The South's licked. If they're going to police a country, let them police the South and send their fighting troops here."

He shook his leonine head and bent forward, grasped both arms of the chair and peered at her through the cigar haze. "It doesn't do any good to talk about it, anyway. You'll get so sick of hearing about Indians by the time this week's out you'll be glad not to mention them, like I am."

They went into the parlor and were sitting down when outside in the warm night a party of riders galloped by with a sudden clatter of shod hooves. The sound made all her tenseness come back. Caleb listened for a moment, then settled back, gazing at his daughter.

"That goes on all the time too."

Before she could answer they both heard the muffled sound of men talking beyond the door and spurs striking the boardwalk. Caleb got up heavily and crossed the room with a heavy stride, threw open the door and peered out.

"Mike, come in, boy."

15

Elizabeth arose and stood waiting. Mike Leary she remembered from years back. It gave her a strange sensation, knowing he was here in the house, for she had loved him breathlessly when she'd been eighteen.

"Elizabeth!"

"Hello, Mike."

He was as ruddy as ever, only now he had a tawny yellow mustache. It went well with his bold blue eyes, his wide shoulders and his capable, slightly unkempt look. He had always looked so dashing, so romantic and strong and tall to her. He still did.

Mike removed his hat and bent from the waist. His bold glance missed nothing in its upward sweep. "Elizabeth, you are positively beautiful. I heard you were back. I had to stop by."

"Thank you. And you are as dashing as ever. Sit down."

Caleb watched them both from behind a facial facade of stony impassiveness. When he cleared his throat and laid aside his cigar the younger man turned toward him. Elizabeth felt a sudden stiffness in the room. She looked at her father but read nothing there. Mike was erect in his chair as though aware of the peculiar atmosphere.

"The Army's bringing in three immigrant wagons under escort. Not a soul saved."

Caleb Mellon glowered at the fireplace for a moment before he spoke. Elizabeth heard the resentment in her father's voice. She guessed from the look on his face and their recent conversation how he felt about having things like this invade the serenity of his house.

"Sioux or Cheyennes, of course."

"Yes, of course. We got there a good two hours late—as usual. We did get a brace of wounded bucks the others didn't haul away."

"What did you do with them?"

16

"Army's got 'em in one of the wagons. One'll never make it. He's gut-shot. The other one's in better shape, but I think his ribs are all broken on the left side."

Elizabeth was shocked at Mike's bluntness. It would take a little time to get used to this kind of people again. "Where did it happen, Mike? Was it immigrants?"

His glance swung swiftly to her face as though awaiting an opportunity to do so. "Happened between here and Ten-Mile. They were immigrant wagons but freighters were using them. Some of Jake Harter's men. There were four Army women with 'em. Going to Ten-Mile where their husbands were." Leary wagged his head at her. "It was a mess."

"All right," her father said quickly. "What's the Army want me to do with the wagons?"

"They got an idea, Caleb. They want 'em sided up with oak under the canvas, and fitted with rifle slits."

Caleb listened, looking interested. Mike Leary swung reluctantly back toward him.

"They want the sideboards made of three inch oak so's they'll turn a bullet or an arrow; then they're going to fill them with soldiers and go Indian hunting."

Elizabeth was only half listening. It had been a Harter train. There, but for the grace of God . . . She shuddered.

"It can be done, all right, but if the Army wants to fight Indians all it's got to do is ride west of us fifty miles and it'll have all the Indian fighting it'll want."

"Not strong enough," Mike Leary said knowingly. "They dassn't risk an all-out fight. Might get whipped, and if they did it'd be worse'n ever—even in the towns then, Caleb. What they want is to ambush this particular bunch that's making the trip to Ten-Mile just about impossible."

"Mike," Elizabeth said softly, "why don't they attack people on all the roads? Why just the Ten-Mile road?"

17

"That's simple," Leary said with a bold smile and a steady look. "They've been trying to gut that fort up there for two years now. They've tried burning it, overwhelming it, tunneling under it even, all without any luck. Now they've gotten wise at last. They're simply sealing it off so's no supplies can get to the people up there. That means the Ten-Mile road, Liz. Starve out the soldiers or make them use up their ammunition. After that . . ." He made a circling motion around his tousled blond head, then, with a graphic jerk, simulated tugging off the scalp.

Caleb's eyes darkened. His face screwed down tightly. He stood up. "All right, Mike. Are you going by the works?"

Mike arose too. "I can, Caleb."

"I'd appreciate it if you'd stop in and pass the word to the foreman. You know him—Lew Dollarhide. Tell him to park those wagons up close in the yard, behind the shop. Ask him to get all the particulars from the Army people and write them down for me. Will you do that?"

"Glad to," Mike said. Then with a rippling movement he swung back toward Elizabeth and said, "There's going to be a dance in Flannery's warehouse, Liz. Would you go with me? It's tomorrow night."

She was undecided. Mike persisted. She saw the storm clouds gathering on her father's face and gave in suddenly. She saw Mike to the door, through it, and closed it behind him.

Caleb was his serene self when she came back into the parlor. He looked at her cryptically, shook his head in silence, then dropped down into the chair again.

"You used to like Mike, Dad," she said.

"I won't say I don't like him now, Liz. He just irritates me is all. That business of imitating scalping

18

someone—now that's not the kind of thing you do in front of ladies, is it?"

She laughed quietly and looked rueful. "I'm not sure I know any more. People seem different to me now."

Caleb squinted at her. Defensively he said, "Well, this isn't the East, honey, and what I've seen of Easterners out here—I thank the Lord it isn't. Anyway, folks're living with their hearts in their mouths nowadays. You've got to understand that."

"I do, Dad. It's just that being dropped down in the middle of a war so suddenly is rather startling."

"Sure it is. Before you're through with it you'll be as sick of it as I am, too."

Musingly she said, "Jacob Harter has a lot of wagons, hasn't he?"

"More than any of the other freighters. Why?"

"Why would he send out immigrant wagons then?"

"Oh, that was an idea he had. The Indians're particularly fierce on freighters going up by Ten-Mile. He thought he'd try immigrant wagons. It was a pretty useless thing, but something's got to be done for those people. There are even women and kids up there, Liz."

"It just doesn't seem real—only ten miles away."

"That's half a day's travel on a good horse or a full day's travel with a freighter. It might just as well be a hundred miles, or two hundred miles. Look at it like that and you'll grasp how hard it is for supplies to be taken up there. It isn't a paved road, either." He got up and stood wide-legged. "Doggoned Indians. Your first day home, too. Well, good night, honey."

She went to her bedroom, just beginning to grasp how serious and how close the Sioux War was to her.

19

CHAPTER II

THE DANCE IN FLANNERY'S WAREHOUSE WAS A seasonal affair. Every Christmas they had one. There was another dance in the spring, then one in midsummer, and, of course, the fall or harvest dance. No one would miss going. Even the very old and the young rambunctious ones were there. The men greased their hair and their boots, the ladies were slightly pop-eyed from constricting corsets, and the young people alone were honestly free to enjoy themselves.

Elizabeth was swamped with attention. Mike Leary wore a strained look of good-natured acceptance, but his eyes flashed every time she was claimed for a dance. His patience, never reliable, was fast wearing thin. Impulsive, a little loud, inclined to swagger and wax his tawny mustache, Mike Leary was a boy grown tall, but still a boy.

Twice she saw Jess Swindin in the crowd of dancers and each time it was with a different girl. He nodded once to her, and she nodded back just as primly. Then, just as Shan Flannery Junior was handing her back to her seat and the little clutch of teamsters, riders and envious girls was closing in, a big frame loomed up, bent over, and a pair of steady grey eyes were close to her face.

"May I have the next dance, Miss Mellon?"

"It's taken," Mike Leary said shortly, looking boldly into Jess Swindin's face. The scout straightened up, gazed at Mike and smiled a little. "Sorry," he said, then let his glance linger before he turned back to Elizabeth. "The one after that, then?"

Angry at Mike—the dance hadn't been taken at all—she said, "Yes."

20

When the music started Mike whirled her out with a great flourish. His face was red and shiny, his eyes bright.

"Liz, you're the prettiest girl here. Even strangers notice it."

She looked at his flushed, proud face and said, "Is that why you want to monopolize me, Mike?"

"You came with me, doggone it. I deserve a few dances, don't I?"

"You've had four," she said matter-of-factly.

"Well, that don't give outlanders a right to bust in, does it?"

"He's no stranger. That's Mr. Harter's scout."

"The one you came from the Missouri with?"

Piqued again, she said, "Mike, I didn't come from Missouri with him and I don't like the way you said that."

He retreated swiftly. "Didn't mean anything, Liz."

But he did and she knew it, because after the dance, while they were waiting for the music to start up again, Mike's antagonistic glance sought out and clung to Jess Swindin as he strolled over toward them. When the music started Mike stonily watched them glide away.

Jess was a smooth dancer. He smiled at her. "You're the belle of the shindig, Miss Mellon."

"I've been away two years, you know."

He looked past her at the other people and said, "It's different, isn't it?"

"What is?"

"The people, the country—all of it."

She studied his calm expression closely. "Were you an Easterner?"

The grey eyes lowered. "Yes," he said, "once. A long time ago. Sometimes it seems like it was a hundred

21

years ago." As smoothly as he danced, he veered the conversation away from further discussion of the topic. "This is better country, though. Even at its worst, it's a lot better. When the Indians are whipped people'll flock out here."

"*When* they're whipped or *if* they're whipped?"

"You don't doubt that they will be, do you?"

She shook her head wearily. "I don't know. That's all I've heard for the last two days—Indians. Some people don't think we'll ever whip them. They say there'll be a compromise. They stay west of the settlements and we'll stay where we are."

"No," he said, "that won't work. They had a treaty at Fort Laramie in 1868, remember? Red Cloud wouldn't sign it until the Army tore down its forts, pulled up its tracks and removed its soldiers. Even made the trappers and miners get out. You know what happened after that, don't you?"

"Vaguely. I didn't pay too much attention, then."

"Too many whites clamoring for the Indians' hunting grounds. Back East they called it Manifest Destiny. The Indians said it was a plain and outright breach of the treaty. Anyway, people came thicker'n ever and rode all over Indian country. What happened next is what we're living through now. War."

"Who's right?" she said. "Surely we own this country."

His eyes sparkled down at her in a tolerant, teasing way. "Both sides are always right in every war, didn't you know that?"

She canted her head a little. "If you don't want to tell me your ideas on that subject, maybe you'd answer one question for me."

"Glad to."

"Did you see any hostiles when you were scouting for Mr. Harter's freighters, while I was along?"

"Yes'm, twice. We ducked them both times because they were ahead of us. If they'd been trailing us—we wouldn't have."

"Thank you."

"No thanks due. Jacob didn't want you upset any more'n he wanted his wagons attacked."

With a sardonic little grin she said, "You kept me from appreciating just how bad conditions are out here. It's made it all the harder for me to grasp things, now that I'm home."

"Well," he said slowly, "sometimes it's better to figure things out in the shade of your front porch than it is from inside an attached freight wagon. Anyway, you'll hear a lot more as time goes on."

"Did you hear about Mr. Harter's immigrant wagons being attacked last night?"

"Yes'm. They brought back most of the bodies and one live buck. In fact, I'm supposed to go down and talk to him in the morning. He's hurt inside and has five busted ribs."

"Can you speak their language?"

"Sign-language, yes. I'm not at all good at their tongue-language." He paused a moment, looking down at her. "Would you like to come with me when I talk to this buck?"

She felt a quick uneasiness. "Well, I don't know that . . ."

"Sure not," he said abruptly. "I'm sorry; I shouldn't have asked."

Her blue eyes flashed. "I'd love to. Will you pick me up at my father's house?"

He had the same distant look of appraisal when he

answered her. "I reckon it isn't the place for a lady—the hospital cell of the town jailhouse."

The glint of her gaze grew harder. "What time will you be by?"

"At nine," he said.

The music stopped and they stood slightly apart; then he wheeled her and strode back to where Mike Leary stood. Jess handed her down on the bench, bowed very slightly, and walked away without a glance at Mike and the others.

Elizabeth went home two dances later. She was tired and Mike had become tiring. When they parted at the front gate Mike gave his mustache a tawny pull and a flourishing sweep. His bold stare was warm.

"Liz, I'll be gone for a couple of days, but when I come back I'd admire a lot to come calling."

If she hadn't known, instinct would have warned her what he meant. "We'll always be glad to see you, Mike," she said, with emphasis on the first word. "Thank you very much for a wonderful time, and good night." She left him like that, went up to the door, paused, stole a quick glance backwards and saw his shadow growing smaller up the boardwalk. She also saw something else. The tall, lanky silhouette of a man standing down by the gate where she and Mike had been, held her motionless. Her heart made a slugging pulse-beat in the vein at her throat. She knew that outline—Harter's scout.

"Ma'am?" It came very softly.

She turned fully and looked annoyed, waiting.

He put one big hand on the gate and opened it, hesitating. "Can I come up?"

"Yes."

He did, with a light, rolling gait. When he was close

24

she saw that he was bareheaded and the moonlight splashed off the reddish tint of his auburn hair. His face was tilted a little, and shadowed. His eyes were wide but hard to see in the dim light.

"I followed you." It sounded like a confession, the way he said it.

"I believe you," she said stiffly.

"Well, I only half did, really. I was walking back to the bunkhouse at Harter's when I saw you and that cowboy ahead of me. I sort of hung around until he left."

"Why? Do you want to go back on your invitation to the jailhouse tomorrow?"

"No," he said drawlingly, "not that. I wondered if you'd take a little walk with me. It's a cool night with a full moon—almost—and I'm not the least bit tired and thought if you weren't we could sort of stroll a little."

"It's late." What she thought was that her feet hurt.

"Just a little walk."

"All right. It is a beautiful night, isn't it?"

They walked south. Around them Clybourne was still alive and lighted. There were other strollers, too, who didn't see them at all in their preoccupation. The night was warm, the stars overhead were like congealed tears cast at random across a firmament of royal blue. The scent in the air was of drying things: grass, sage, oily leaves, juniper trees and willow buds. It was benevolently warm, too, showing that even without the smashing sunlight the earth and air still held heat.

They spoke of general things until they came to the bench outside her father's buggy works, where Jess Swindin made a swipe with his handkerchief and they both sat down. He turned sideways on the bench and looked at her.

25

"You're wondering why I wanted to see you. I'll tell you. There aren't many people here I like to talk to."

"You don't know me well enough to say you like to talk to me."

"No, but you're different. You've just come back here. You'd understand—whether you talked back or not." He looked beyond her with a brooding expression. "Ever feel like you'd like to talk to someone badly enough to make a nuisance out of yourself to do it?"

"I don't think so," Elizabeth said. "At least I can't recall if I have."

"That's how I've felt ever since we danced together."

"It took a long time for you to think that."

He squirmed on the bench. "You mean the trip from the Missouri. That was different. It would've started the others talking. Besides, I had a notion you might be stuck up after being back East. I didn't decide you weren't until we got back to Clybourne."

"Are you sure now?"

"Yes." The answer was as direct as his glance. "I'm sure now." He slumped. "Were you in New York?"

"For two months. I've two aunts there."

"Tell me about it."

"You're the one that wanted to talk. I'm a good listener." She was vastly curious about him. He wasn't just a scout or a freighter or a cowboy; about that much she'd made up her mind. His English was better; his features were, too. There was something magnetically sad about him.

"And Chicago?"

"Yes, I stayed there the longest. My father's brother and his family live there."

His head came up a little. He didn't look at her but gazed over the town with its little trickles of orange-

26

yellow lantern light lying in the roadway dust from dozens of curtained windows.

"You walked along the lake-front, you went to the opera house and out on the sand-dunes, you rode the horse-cars and ate fried fish and visited the park and the zoo."

"You know Chicago," she said, watching his profile.

"Yes, I know the place. Maybe you went out to the ball park. Not many ladies do, though. I'll bet you ducked the pigeons, and in the evenings went to the outdoor band concerts. The musicians're usually Dutchmen with red suspenders and brass horns."

He talked on in his calm, even way, and for a moment she felt a distinct nostalgia for Chicago, although while she'd been there she hadn't cared for the town at all.

She folded her hands in her lap and leaned back, looking at the sky. He was a strange person, quick and solid in a lean, pantherish way, and there was a constant flow of energy that emanated from him even when he sat still and relaxed as now. She looked around finally, when his voice died away.

"Why don't you go back? You love it; I can tell from the way you talk."

"No, I don't love it. I miss it, but I don't love it." He pushed himself upright on the bench and craned his neck northward. Clybourne's lamps were dwindling one by one. He swung to face her. "It takes time to forget it all."

"You didn't leave it voluntarily, though."

"No, you're right."

"A woman," she said.

His gaze seemed to darken. "You're fishing. That isn't ladylike."

"Neither is sitting here after midnight."

27

"But you are a lady." His face was expressionless. Even so she got the impression it was a question.

"Yes, I'm a lady." She let it lie there for a moment, then spoke again. "It was a woman, wasn't it?"

He leaned back again without looking at her. "What makes you think that?"

"You didn't play cards with the other men in the freight train. You haven't smelt of liquor since I've been around you. You aren't a gunman or a drifter, particularly."

"So that leaves a woman?"

He was mocking her and she knew it. "To a man like you—yes."

"What kind of a man is that?"

She looked out over the town again, but there was a tiny pucker between her eyes. "I've learned one thing about you tonight. You're a genius for switching the subject when you want to."

He chuckled for the first time, and their eyes met and held. He had a roguish twinkle in his glance. "You're very observant, Elizabeth, along with being pretty. Do me a favor, will you? Don't dig too deep."

Annoyed, she said, "Maybe we'd better go back now."

He didn't move, but his head dropped a little and the sparkle died out gradually until his face was impassive, as relaxed and aloof as ever.

Withdrawn, she thought. He lived within a shell of his own making.

"All right," he said tonelessly, still making no move to arise. "When's the next dance?"

Surprised by the irrelevancy of it, she said, "In September, I think. It's the harvest dance."

"Will you save that for me?"

28

"That's two months off."

"You don't have to be evasive," he said quietly. "Yes or no will be good enough. Anyway, I might not be around to take you. It's an even bet you won't have to go with me if you don't want to."

Borrowing a trick from him, she sidestepped the issue with a question. "Are you moving on?"

"Not exactly," he said dryly. "Remember what Jacob said about getting the Army's stuff to Ten-Mile, the day we pulled into Clybourne? Well, I'm going out with them tomorrow. If it doesn't happen tomorrow it'll happen one of these days. Like Jake's always piping about—the odds're against freighters and their outriders."

"Oh." She remembered with a rush. For a while she had forgotten the frontier and its bloody sunsets and conditions of siege.

"It would be something to look forward to."

"I'll go with you, of course."

He leaned forward with both hands on his knees and looked critically at her. "Because you're feeling sorry for me? You don't have to. No one makes me outride. I do it because I like to."

"That's not very sensible," Elizabeth said.

"You'd be surprised," he said, rising, standing there tall and shadowy, gazing at her. "It's not as bad as people imagine. There's danger, sure, but as long as you aren't alone there's a chance you'll come back. For that reason you don't have to worry. It's the off-chance that'll do it, if anything ever does."

"What do you mean by 'the off-chance'?"

"A lucky shot. A knife in the night. An ambush. Things that might catch any of us off guard sometime. With hostile Indians it's usually fatal."

29

She got up and walked beside him. The moonlight cast their shadows into the dust of the roadway just off the boardwalk. Neither of them said anything until they were back to Mellon's gate; then he opened it and walked her up to the door, stood back and took a last long look at her.

"Do you like flattery, Elizabeth?"

She answered him with a little uncertainty in her voice. "Yes, everyone does."

"You are the handsomest woman I've seen in six years."

"Thank you." She felt for the door latch, lifted it and smiled at him. "At nine o'clock in the morning?"

"Later if you'd rather."

"Nine o'clock. Good night."

They parted with the dying lights of Clybourne around them and the far-off cry of a coyote making a melancholy, lonely sound, that drew some drowsy answers from the town dogs.

At nine o'clock he came by for her. She was waiting alone, her father having departed much earlier for the buggy works. Intuitively, she had some hot coffee ready when he knocked, greeted him genially and handed him a cup of it. It was black and strong. He took two long swallows and blinked at her.

"It's good, mind—best coffee I've had today—but you could float a horseshoe in it."

"I thought all strong men liked strong coffee."

Lazily he said, "I like strong coffee, but I reckon you overappraised my strength." Then he smiled at her quickly and added, "You never made a bad cup of coffee in your life. I like to tease people first thing in the morning."

30

She put aside the cups and gave her hair a final pat. It was wavy with a sheen to it, like spun copper. "One would never guess it to look at you. You're actually rather cold and forbidding-looking."

He didn't answer that.

Outside, the sun had already overwhelmed the land, running down over it like a molten river of brass. The reflections stung the eyes and made them water. A faint, dying smell of the earlier hours still lingered, but the sun was dissipating. People were abroad. Women hurried with poke-bonnets and shawls over their heads, to get their outside work done before the heat became unbearable. Men walked with more restraint, or were gathered together in little knots, talking. At the far south end of town a whirling dust cloud jerked to life under the hooves of a hard-riding party of wild-looking men. Jess squinted from beneath his hat and Elizabeth heard his quick intake of breath. She shot a look at the oncoming riders and up at his face.

"What's the matter?"

He didn't answer right away, and when he did, he didn't take his eyes off the slowing men, who were now engulfed in dust of their own making.

"Trouble."

"Who are they?"

"That I don't know," he answered tersely.

"Then how do you know it's trouble?"

That made him look around and down at her. "See those three horses without saddles?"

"Yes."

"Well, look closer at them."

Then she understood. Three of the horses the strangers had ridden into town had harness stains on them, but no harness. They were big brutes, heads down

31

and worn out, but definitely wagon horses. The fact that they were ridden meant they'd been taken out of their harnesses somewhere out on the plains.

"Indians, Jess?"

"They'll do it every time. Attack right at dawn. Lie there all night waiting for the first streak of light, studying things, then—wham—come in like the wind!"

At the jailhouse a harsh silence fell when Jess pointedly stood aside for Elizabeth to enter. The atmosphere was sulphurous with quickly throttled profanity. Jacob Harter and three other men she knew were in the room. The other seven men were all strangers. One had caked, crusted blood down both sides of his shirt, front and back, and a mangled ear.

Jacob cast a disapproving look at Jess but greeted Elizabeth with a nod and motioned them through the little door beyond the main room. "He's still alive. Even eats a little now. Do what you want with him."

Jess nodded at the strangers and stopped long enough to look inquiringly at Jacob. The freighter shook his head. "Later," he said, still looking nettled that Jess had brought Elizabeth down there.

They went through the partitioning door and Jess closed it tightly behind them. Instantly the voices erupted again in the outer room, but they were being held low so the words didn't filter through.

Elizabeth sniffed at the odors of the cell-block and stood closer to Jess. She didn't see the buck Indian until Jess made a motion toward the strap-steel cell with the door hanging open.

Jess walked into the cell, stopped close to the bunk and looked dispassionately at the brown, tawny figure sprawled with lifeless stillness there. There was a hand-forged leg-iron riveted to the warrior's ankle. His side had been clumsily, reluctantly bandaged. His eyes were black and sunken far back in his head. His mouth was wide, thin-lipped and set.

Elizabeth moved closer. Without a word Jess swiveled his head, saw a little horseshoe-nail keg, got it from against the wall and set it down by her.

"Sit down, Elizabeth. This'll take a little time. No sense in standing up through it."

She sat, terrified by the intensely black stare of the wounded Indian. There was a strong, musty odor in the little cell. She wasn't sure whether it was caused by the Indian or not.

Jess turned to her and made a sign as though cutting his own throat with the edge of his right hand drawn across his gullet. "Sioux," he said. "He's a Sioux warrior."

He turned back and repeated the motion to the Indian. For a space of blank, watchful seconds the buck didn't respond; then he made the same throat-cutting motion to affirm what Jess said. He was a Sioux.

Jess closed his right fist with the thumb touching the index finger, held it thus for a moment, then flexed the finger outward in a snapping gesture and pointed it, moving forward, toward the Sioux.

The Indian's eyes began to lose a little of their glazed look. He looked Jess up and down, then said aloud, "Wambdi Ska."

"Means White Eagle," Jess said in English.

The Sioux then put his right hand palm outward in front of his chest and flipped it over, then returned it to the former position, hesitated, then lifted it to his mouth and moved it, held flat, out and back several times. Then he used both hands, fingers cupped, to make simultaneous movements down his body and back,

33

halfway up his chest again. He finished his *wibluta* signs with his right hand held at his bandaged side, first finger extended. He brushed the bandages with the extended finger, wiggling his hand as he did so. After that he stared steadily at Jess.

"What did he say?"

"Well, literally he said 'no talk—much hurt.' What he means is that he's hurt too badly to talk much. I suppose he is, with broken ribs." Jess gazed at Elizabeth, then hunkered down beside her. "I'm going to ask him if a strong wagon train could get through to Ten-Mile."

Jess put his right hand even with his shoulder, fingers upward and apart. He then twisted it a little from right to left. "Question." Now he used both hands, slightly cupped, and moved them down his body and brought them back up again, halfway. "Many." Next, with both fists clenched and held in front of his chest, the right hand down by elbow action so that the knuckles barely touched the knuckles of his motionless left fist. "Brave."

Now he paused a second, watching the motionless Sioux, before he placed both hands in front of him a foot or so, cupped them both but left the first two fingers free and bent inward. Then he brought both hands back toward his chest simultaneously, making the rolling motions of a wagon wheel. "Wagons." For the word "go," he simply used his right hand, open, palm outward at chest level, and pushed it outward, fingers slanting down a little.

Saying "fort" in sign-language was involved. First, the sign "white." Jess pointed to the grey-white wall. Next the sign for "man." The right index finger held upward, fingernail out away from face. Then the sign for "house." The fingers of both hands interlocked at the tips and held horizontally on front of the chest.

34

The warrior raised his right hand shoulder high and wiggled it by the wrist. "Question." Then he held up both hands, fingers upright, palms outward. "Ten." Next, with his right fist loosely closed, he held it sideways in front of his right side and pushed it upwards about six or eight inches. "Mile."

Jess said, "Yes," by holding his right hand, first finger erect, just below his right shoulder, then bringing it downward and to the left at the same time.

White Eagle's wasted face shone with a malevolent light. His eyes glittered triumphantly. He put his left hand in front of his chest, palm upward, and with a very definite and angry motion, he swung the right hand, palm downward, across it. He repeated this motion several times with great relish.

Elizabeth was impressed both with his sign-talk and the way he glowered at Jess. "What does that mean?"

"It means anyone who tries it will be wiped out. That's the *wibluta* sign for wiping out, exterminating."

He turned back and his hands flew in graceful movement, but the Indian made the signs for "no more—no talk white man; no good," and closed his eyes and turned his head away when Jess persisted. Arising, looking baffled and unfriendly, Jess traded dark looks with the wounded buck. Then Elizabeth stood up too.

"Don't, Jess. Let's leave him alone."

They went back out into the office. Jacob and the town marshal were there. Only some small, irregular dark spots on the floor showed that others had been in the room. Jacob's eyes lifted to Jess' face. His expression was worried and his glance troubled.

"What'd you get out of him?"

"Nothing. Only that anyone who tries getting to Ten-Mile will be wiped out."

"Nothing new in that," the marshal said, then got up and stumped back through the cell-block door.

Harter looked from Jess to Elizabeth, then beyond to the wall. His mouth was sucked flat. "They've got to roll, Jess."

"I'm ready."

"I know," Jacob said flatly. "Maybe the Indians are too. They know we've got to get help to Ten-Mile."

Elizabeth ventured a question. "Who were those men in here when we came down, Mr. Harter?"

"Them?" Jacob said in a distant, disinterested way. "More wagoneers who were jumped at dawn." His head came up. "In a way it's our fault, too. They were following our tracks from day before yesterday—and so was a big war party."

"How many killed?" Jess asked.

"Eleven and the wagons burnt. Seven teamsters cut loose and rode for it. Every one made it. They said it was a band of over two hundred warriors." His dry-looking eyes fixed themselves on Jess' face. He spoke of what was uppermost in his mind.

"According to Shan Flannery, who sent up the last load of supplies, Ten-Mile can't last more'n two days."

There was a thick silence after that. Elizabeth felt as though a hand were squeezing her heart. She moved toward a vacant chair and eased down in it. Jess stood slouched, wide-legged. Jacob was hanging on the edge of a messy table, his left leg dangling, head up and eyes unblinking, unseeing.

Jess said, "Are you going with me, Jake?"

"Sure. They're my wagons."

"You'll be wagon-master, then."

Jacob looked irritated. "What difference does that make?"

36

"Not much," Jess said. Turning away, he crossed the room and sank down on a wall bench.

"Mr. Harter, can I make him some gruel?" Elizabeth asked.

Jacob looked up, bewildered. "Who? Jess?"

"No, the Indian."

"Feed him?" Harter said. "Feed him?" He jumped off the table and struck the floor hard with his booted left leg. "I'll feed him, dang his black hide. I'll feed him bullets until he'll sink!" He flung out of the little office. Jess looked across at her understandingly.

"He's upset, Elizabeth. He didn't mean to be rude, but if I were you I'd soft-pedal kindly talk where Indians are concerned, right now."

"I can see that," she said.

"Now you know why I balked. Let's go back."

She swung in beside him on the boardwalk and said, "It wasn't your fault. Anyway, Mr. Harter was mad as soon as he saw me walk in with you."

"I know. I saw his face too."

She swung sideways a little as she walked. "Jess, where's the Army? Why isn't something done officially about Ten-Mile?"

"That's where the Army is, Elizabeth; up there. The folks in Clybourne've set out riders to the other Army posts and camps, but Ten-Mile can't wait. Indians caught them between supply and restocking. Smarter'n coyotes. They studied when Ten-Mile would be running low; then they threw down their blockade. That way, you see, even if Army help was hurried right up there, Ten-Mile'd be starved out before help could arrive."

He made his way through the thin line of other walkers with his head down, his hat shading his eyes.

"I'll bet you those bucks who attacked that wagon

37

train at dawn south of town weren't after plunder. They were down there to intercept and delay any help that might come up here for the fort."

She saw her father on the boardwalk in his shirt-sleeves talking to Jacob Harter and two other men. She scarcely noticed any of them. A blanketing pall of dread was filtering into her consciousness. Harter had said it was war. He had been right, but not totally right. It was war with the enemy winning.

"Elizabeth!"

She stopped, as did Jess. Her father looked from one of them to the other. She spoke listlessly. "Dad, this is Jess Swindin."

Jess nodded. "We know each other." But he offered his hand anyway, and Caleb Mellon grasped it fleetingly, then dropped it. His face wasn't very genial. There was storminess in his eyes and a harassed expression around his mouth.

"You had no business down there, Liz." He said it to her, but his eyes lay gratingly on Jess. The scout shot a short glance at Jacob and the other two men, whom he recognized as two of Jacob's wagon-masters off northward runs, before he spoke quietly to Caleb.

"I'm sorry. I shouldn't have taken her up there."

"I wanted to go, Dad. I'm not sorry I did—exactly."

Her father's gaze drifted to his shimmering gate down the road a few hundred feet. Pointedly he said, "Jess, when you've walked her home, come back up here, will you?"

They continued on their way, and Elizabeth was furious. "If he says a word to you, you tell him I asked you to take me down there to see that Indian."

"Sure," Jess said placatingly. "Listen to me for a minute. Don't be like the rest of them; don't let your nerves turn into white worms that eat you up. That's

38

what's the matter with the whole country right now, Elizabeth. Nerves. Indian nerves; war nerves—call it what you want, but don't succumb to it."

"But he only said that to get me out of the way while he tongue-lashes you."

"Maybe," he said, reaching for the gate hasp, springing it and holding the gate back for her to pass beyond. "Maybe so. I wouldn't blame him, if you were my daughter. Anyway, I don't mind. Everyone's as jumpy as a cat nowadays."

"But you," she said. "You're not."

"I make it a point not to listen to their imaginings nor to get as excited as they are." He smiled winningly at her. "Try it; it's like living in another world."

She let the anger wither and stood there in the murderous sun looking up at him. He had a strong, appealing personality. She couldn't have disliked him if she'd tried, and she didn't try.

"Well, when are you going out with the wagons?"

"Late tonight, if I can talk sense into Jacob."

"Oh." She stood looking at him with an idea in mind. Very deliberately she said, "Would you come to supper tonight?"

It jolted him. His eyes wavered even before he spoke. "You're being kind. Listen, I'm not the least bit worried about what your father will say to me. Don't make an issue of it by ramming me down his throat across the supper table. That isn't good for any of us."

"I'm not asking you to spite my father. I'm asking you because you'll be riding out afterward."

He almost blurted out, "Oh, a farewell dinner," but he caught himself in time and stood soberly gazing across the gate at her. Even with a flushed face she was startlingly handsome.

"I'd love to. What time?"

They agreed on seven; then he swung back up toward the buggy works with a long, free and purposeful stride.

CHAPTER III

CALEB MELLON AND JACOB HARTER WERE ALONE when Jess got back. Behind them the hammering and machinery of the buggy works was close to deafening. Elizabeth's father watched the long stride of the approaching younger man and stirred himself.

"Let's go over to Nolan's. Can't hear yourself think in here."

With a nod that indicated acquiescence to Caleb Mellon, and indicated their direction to Jess, Jacob Harter scuffled through the heavy dust of the roadway, beside the buggy-maker.

Inside Nolan's *Union Jack Saloon,* Mellon nodded three times at the barman, and three glasses of tepid ale appeared. Jess was the last one up to the bar. He watched the bubbles rise in the brew, but Jacob Harter, with a flat hand depressing his beard, drank deeply. Mellon took two swallows and set his mug down, hard.

"Get anything out of that Indian, Jess?"

"No."

"Made a sorry sight, I imagine."

"He did."

They both understood the innuendoes. The topic was closed as far as Elizabeth's father was concerned.

Jacob was watching his second ale come at him with a moody expression. Now he turned sideways and leaned on the bar, looking past Mellon toward Swindin.

"A Sioux?"

Jess nodded, knowing how Harter's mind ran.

"Part of a big band, I suppose."

More silence.

Jacob grunted and shifted his gaze to Caleb Mellon. "How many tin soldiers still in town, Caleb?"

"Sixteen."

That time Jacob's sound was a snort. "Sixteen tin soldiers and they want an armored wagon to hunt Indians with. That's downright childish."

"I don't know, Jacob. The lieutenant was in again this morning. He's been rounding up volunteer recruits among the townsmen. He's sweating over Ten-Mile. He's hell-bent to try, anyway."

"They won't get five miles out of Clybourne; not three miles."

"Don't bet on it, Jacob. He said he had two hundred townsmen ready to go along."

"Well," Jacob said, suddenly mollified, "that's different."

Jess spoke for the first time since Jacob had started talking. "How long before you'll have that wagon ready?"

"Be late, Jess. Maybe sundown or later."

"That's fine," Jess said, avoiding Jacob's questioning look.

Jacob protested as Jess thought he would. "Sundown, nothin'!" he said. "I don't want to hang around until it's too dark to see, Indians or no Indians."

Jess sipped his beer and spoke without looking at his employer. "Jacob, why don't you go talk that soldier into bringing his men along with us, then get things lined up to start as soon as Mr. Mellon's through arming the wagon?"

"It'll be too late, Jess. You heard what Caleb said."

Caleb interrupted with a ponderous shake of his shaggy head. "I can't get those oak liners under that canvas short of four hours, boys. That's all there is to it."

Speaking swiftly, to cut off more protests by Jacob, Jess said: "Be better if we didn't start until after dark anyway."

Harter's dour look grew deeper, more settled and stubborn. "I don't like night traveling even if it is easier on the stock this time of the year. The Indians . . ."

"The Indians won't fight at night if they can help it," Jess said flatly. "Their religion is against it. You know that, Jacob. Besides, they're bad enough marksmen during the day. At night they can't hit the broad side of a barn."

Jacob made a wry face. "They hit my Conestogas last night, Jess."

The grey eyes went back down to a thoughtful consideration of the ale bubbles and stayed there. Jess said nothing.

Mellon squinted at him. "Well? How about that, Jess?"

"What about it? In the first place, whoever was Jacob's outrider must have been asleep. I don't like to say that; the man's dead, but whoever he was—if he'd been sniffing like he should've been, it would've been a fight—not necessarily a massacre."

"How do you know what happened?" Jacob asked harshly.

"I saw that wagon come back—the one Mellon's arming."

Jacob's bitter look didn't lessen. He lapsed into glum silence again.

Jess went on. "I think a strong train of even-numbered wagons could get through to Ten-Mile."

Mellon said, "How?" in a doubting tone of voice.

"Make the run after dark. Have a strong guard of outriders. Use that armored wagon in the rear. That's where they always sweep in close for killing shots."

Jacob was idly twisting his beer mug, staring at the consecutive damp circles. Caleb Mellon was leaning on the bar with his chin in one hand, gazing vacantly at his own reflection in the back-bar mirror.

"There's a couple of other twists a man might try, too."

Without raising his head Jacob Harter said: "Such as?"

"How many wagons are going, Jacob?"

"Nine freighters loaded with Army goods, and the armored one makes ten."

"Good; there should be an even number of them."

Jacob looked up finally. His face was baffled as he gazed over at Jess. "Go on; I'm no mindreader."

Jess ran his hand through the water under his beer mug, raised one wet finger and made a triangle that was open at the lower end. Each side of the triangle had five wet marks to outline it. "Wagons," he explained. "Five on each side. Armored Conestoga at the very back. Which side it's on doesn't make any difference, just so long as it's in the rear for support when the Indians try to smash into the triangle from the open end."

"Why leave the triangle open?" Jacob asked, looking dispassionately at the damp diagram.

"Jake, you know they always try to kill the teams first, to stop the wagons. Well, we could drive fifteen or twenty loose replacement horses and mules inside the triangle, where they'd be protected."

Jess drew his damp finger across the open end of the triangle, closing it tightly. "We'll put every mounted

43

man back there that we don't need as outriders, to hold that open end. They'll keep the corraled animals inside the triangle, and they'll be back there waiting for the Indians."

For a moment all the three of them heard were the falling chips at a distant Black-Jack table where some old gaffers were playing in the shadows. Then an incautious blue-tail fly blundered into a spider's web and added its frantic buzzing to the silence.

Caleb Mellon looked around at Jacob. The wagon-master was staring unblinkingly at the fading diagram. Mellon spoke to Harter.

"That's the first time I've ever heard anyone suggest a new way to take wagons against the Indians. How's it look to you, Jacob?"

Jacob ignored the question. He said nothing all the while he studied Jess' triangle. Finally he pushed upright on the bar and combed his beard with his fingers and sighed.

"All right. I don't know whether it'll work or not, but it's no worse than the old way of lining 'em out until you smell trouble, then corraling."

Caleb struck the bar with a doubled-up fist. "I've got to get back. Jacob, send up mules to haul that Conestoga down to your corrals, will you?"

"Sure. When do you want them?"

"Sundown."

After Elizabeth's father left, Jacob shuffled over closer to Jess and nodded twice at the barman, then threw a significant glance at Jess' untouched ale.

"Drink her down; another's coming."

Jess drank his first and Jacob downed his third ale, gazed at the empty mug with misty, blank-looking eyes, and said, "I'd better hunt up that tin soldier. I still hate

44

freighting after dark, but I expect it's now or never." He looked up quickly with a calculating expression on his face. "If he'll throw in his sixteen blue-bellies and two hundred townsmen, and if I can get another hundred of my own, Jess, I believe we can make it."

"Use the wagons like a fort on wheels and put that armored Conestoga in back and I'd say we can."

Jacob nodded. "I'll go you one better. You be wagon-boss this trip; I'll take over as scout."

"No," Jess said quickly. "I'd rather scout."

"What's the matter; don't you think I've ever scouted?"

"It's not that, Jacob. I've got the feel for scouting, and I'm no freighter."

"Well," Jacob said, not altogether mollified, "all right—but you line them out the way you got in mind."

"Sure," Jess said. "See you at the corrals in a little while."

"At the cook-shack," Jacob said, turning away.

"No, I'm eating with the Mellons tonight. I'll be down there after supper—about dark, say."

Jacob looked surprised but he didn't show it for long. He turned abruptly and walked toward the louvred doors. Jess watched Jacob's progress all the way across the saloon in the back-bar mirror; then he raised his second mug of ale a little past his lips in a silent salute, and downed it.

He strolled across the road to the buggy works and watched the cursing workmen arming the huge, battered old immigrant wagon. The oaken sideboards were cumbersome and heavy. In the process of refitting the wagon, a new aft near-wheel had been put on it and a new tailgate of solid oak, also. Jess was peering over the tailgate watching the workmen sweat and bolt the

45

wooden armor into place beneath the scorched canvas, when Caleb Mellon came up.

"No arrow will get through that. No bullet either." He had to raise his voice to be heard above the noise of the shop. "The only way they'll breach this wagon will be to fire it."

Jess rocked down on his heels. "If they get close enough to set it afire," he said, "by then the men inside'll be beyond caring."

"What about fire arrows?" Caleb suggested.

"They'll have water. Every wagon carries water for that, nowadays. Anyway, fire arrows aren't especially dangerous unless there's no one inside to see them when they hit."

He left the buggy works shortly after that. For one thing, the noise set up an echoing din inside his head. He wasn't used to it.

He went down to Harter's corrals and found excitement prevalent there too. Even the boy swampers bristled with guns. He went into the log bunkhouse and rummaged for a cake of lye soap. With that he went up the creek behind the corrals and took a bath. Then he dressed. He owned one white shirt and a shoestring tie. He donned both. Suet rubbed lavishly into his boots made them pliable. The added lamp-black gave them a dull shine when he rubbed them briskly. He only owned one hat and it was sweat-streaked, so when he was fully dressed he stood there bareheaded. A craggy-faced Scot teamster poked his head through the door and eyed Jess in surprise for a moment.

"Jake wants ye, Jess—in the office." The little pale eyes flickered over Jess again; then the grizzled head bobbed wonderingly. "Ye'll not be goin' ag'in' them h'athen dressed li' that, will ye?"

46

"No, I'm eating out. I'll change before we pull out, Mac."

He went down to Jacob's tiny office with its piles of broken harness, squeezed inside and sniffed at the strong odor of the place.

Jacob saw him do it and smiled grimly without humor. "Three ales with you and Caleb—and three with the baby-faced tin soldier to humor him until he agreed to throw in with us."

"Did the Army agree?" Jess asked.

"Yes, the Army agreed. Top that off with a full force, including my people here and all the townsmen that'll go—and we've got three hundred and seventeen men. How's that strike you?"

"Just about right," Jess said. "That'll make a lot of extra weight on the wagons that're loaded, but we'll just go slower."

"Yeah—slower. Jess, it isn't the weight that's bothering me. Finding places for them to get out of sight's going to be cussed hard to do."

"It'll be dark."

Jacob snorted. "Sioux can see in the dark when it's an ambush." Then his face brightened and his eyes glittered. "But I'll hide them. I'll get them hid if I have to stand 'em one atop the other and empty a wagon. The Indians're going to learn something tonight, by gosh."

"I hope so," Jess said, moving toward the door. "See you after dark, Jacob."

"Watch your manners."

Clybourne was brimming with muted excitement. He turned in at the Mellon gate, and Elizabeth opened the door and smiled down at him.

Her dark-golden hair was pulled back, but nothing could straighten the waves in it. Her face shone pink

47

from the wood-stove, and there was a still, admiring look moving in the background of her blue eyes. Jess didn't know it, but he made a striking figure.

"Are you always so punctual?"

He smiled and followed her into the house. The aroma of a roast struck him instantly. "For woman-cooked meals I am. Everything else waits."

"Even Indians?"

Caleb Mellon stood up and wagged his head at her. "Indians! Do I have to eat Indians, sleep Indians, talk Indians? Jess, I got the Conestoga done."

Elizabeth moved away from them. "Do I have to eat wagons, sleep wagons, talk wagons?"

Jess laughed, and Caleb smiled at her. "All you have to do is feed us," he said.

"It's ready right now. Go sit down."

They did, but Caleb didn't stop talking until after Elizabeth was at the table too.

"It'll mean three extra teams, Jess. She put on that much weight with the armor. Water casks fore and aft and sawdust on the decking."

"Dad—please!"

"Oh! Yes. Our Father, Make Us Truly Grateful For What We Are About To Receive. Help yourself, Jess. Start the platter going."

"Elizabeth?"

"Thank you. How many men are going?"

Jess quoted Jacob Harter. "Over three hundred."

"What are the odds, do you know?"

"No, but I don't expect there'll be over five hundred. If there're more it'll still be in our favor."

"The armored wagon?"

"That and the darkness. Indians don't like to fight in the dark. Has something to do with a belief that a

48

warrior killed in the night spends Eternity wandering around in the dark."

"That might not be much to depend on," Elizabeth said.

"We're not just depending on that. We'll align the wagons into a formation that'll give us maximum protection and put the warriors at a disadvantage."

"Jess' idea, Liz," Caleb said. "Make a kind of a triangle, with loose-stock inside for replacements when an animal gets downed."

Elizabeth fixed her glance on Jess. "How do you figure odds against Indians?"

Jess grinned crookedly. "A man named Fetterman once said if the Army would give him eighty good troopers he'd ride through the Sioux nation. Fort Fetterman is named after him."

"I remember that," Elizabeth said. "Now give me a straight answer, please."

Jess' grin widened. "I can't say. Some figure it a good gamble at four to one. Others say less than that. I'm inclined to think not more than two-to-one odds against Sioux and Cheyennes in a pitched battle."

"Do you think there'll be less than six hundred Indians?"

"I doubt if it'll be much less; maybe a few more, from what folks say here in town and what Harter's other drivers and scouts say. If there're more, the darkness and the wagons will offset the difference, I think."

"It'll be terribly dangerous," she said.

Caleb raised his head irritably. "Don't keep fretting so, Liz. It isn't a matter of being prepared and ready; it's a case of duty and desperation."

Jess thought Mellon put it very well but he didn't say so.

49

They ate with desultory conversation interspersed through the meal, then went into the parlor. Jess glanced once out the window and saw the shadows lengthening. An hour's daylight remained, maybe less.

"Cigar?"

"No thanks."

Elizabeth sat upright with her hands in her lap. She was tense and it showed. Jess smiled at her.

"You're a little upset over this, Elizabeth. No need to be. There'll be a skirmish, but that's about all."

"How can you be so sure?"

"Just guessing. All things considered, though, I don't expect more than that."

"You're overly optimistic."

"Maybe."

Caleb grunted out of his chair, trailing cigar smoke. "Someone's coming to the door." Neither Jess nor Elizabeth had heard the bootsteps until Caleb remarked on them.

When her father had disappeared down the entryway, Elizabeth sank back in her chair. "It makes me sick thinking about it."

"Remember what I told you? Nerves. If you let them, they'll eat into you like they've eaten into most of the other folks around Clybourne."

"I can't help it."

"Sure you can." He turned his head and looked out the window again. Into the silence came the deep-rumbling tones of men talking just beyond the front door. It was getting murky out. Jess stood up. Elizabeth came up slowly, facing him.

"It was the best meal I've had in years. Thank you very much."

"Jess . . ."

"Yes?"

"Nothing." Her eyes were dark. "Jess, do you think of her?"

"Her?" he said. Then he understood and stood very still gazing back. "Let's not spoil a perfect evening, Elizabeth."

"I'm not. I mean, I don't want to. I'm sorry."

"Good night, Elizabeth."

"Good night and good luck, Jess."

She started to go with him to the door, but he shook his head. "I know where it is."

Outside, the shadows were lowering rapidly. The summer sunset was a memory now. Caleb and a cadaverous-looking man with a brick-red and peeling nose stood to one side as Jess left the house.

"Good night, Mr. Mellon, and thanks for your courtesy."

"Jess, you're welcome, boy. God bless you."

He went down the plank walk after a short nod at the stranger. He was too preoccupied to try and recall where he'd seen the man in the shadows with Elizabeth's father before.

Did he think of her? Yes, as a man thinks of an old wound or a poignant memory, as though he were apart from it, looking down or back on it, seeing it happen all over again, seeing the mistakes they both made; understanding them with a rare wisdom. Yes, he thought of her. Out on the freightways sometimes, when the night was filled with the smell of wild mint or the moon was full enough to wash everything apple-blossom white, he thought of her.

"Jess? Hurry up. Jake's like a flea in a skillet, calling for you every two minutes."

He changed back into his trail clothes. The sweatband

51

of his hat pressing down around his forehead, and the dead-weight sag of the Dragoon pistol nagging at his stride, brought him back to the present.

Men were everywhere. Mostly, they didn't say much. The moonlight reflected off gun barrels, off naked pistols shoved unceremoniously into waistbands, and off tight, set faces.

"Jess!"

"Are the soldiers in the Conestoga, Jacob?"

"Half an hour ago."

"All right; calm down, will you? Let's get the townsmen into the wagons. I'll give positions for the road and we'll roll out."

Jacob's voice sounded flat. "How many do you want as outriders and how many mounted at the back of the triangle?"

"We'll want at least one hundred of them as outriders, Jake. Fifty on each side. Show me the leaders of the men and I'll station the lot of them. For the wagon-ends we won't need more than twenty or so. Just enough to make sure no animals slip out while we're rolling."

"Come along. Shan Flannery's one of the elected bosses. Tell him."

"I'll find him by myself," Jess said. "You get the men into the wagons."

Gradually order of sorts was created out of the milling confusion, but it took a long hour to do it, and in the meantime men and horses were everywhere. When everything was finally ready, Jess was at his scouting position—at the point of the cavalcade. He twisted in his saddle and looked out over the train. It was aligned and shaped. Jacob came loping, his face glistening with perspiration. To forestall him, Jess raised an arm high, wig-wagged it over his head, holding his hat like a flag, then dropped it and sang out a Sioux word they all knew.

"Hoppo!" (Let's go.)

The mules and horses leaned into the harness. The huge wheels ground down into the brick-hard earth. Men called out to one another and to the people who would stay behind. There were a few rough jokes, a little laughter, but not much.

Jess fixed the first rise of land in his mind and held a steady course for it. The north-south road was darker than the grass-carpeted range, but their peculiar wagon formation was far too wide to be accommodated by any roadway. It strung out on both sides like an arrowhead. Jess was at the point. Jacob came in beside him to ride stirrup. His face in the moonlight was grey, his beard almost black.

"You forgot your coat."

Jess looked around. Jacob was holding out his Indian jacket with the bone buttons. He reached for it. The night was warm but the small hours wouldn't be.

"Thanks. How's it look back down there?"

"Looks good. Thing is, as I see it, not to let them breach the triangle."

"Everybody knows that, I reckon. In that respect we're no different from a regular train."

"No," Jacob said. "But that open end back there looks like our weak spot. Caleb Mellon's in charge of it."

Jess' face turned in the soft light and stared. Without raising his voice or showing the astonishment he felt, he said, "Is he with us? I left him standing outside the front door of his house in town."

"He's with us. Him and Dollarhide, his foreman."

Then Jess remembered where he'd seen the lanky individual Mellon had been talking to. He slumped a

53

little. "No sense in him coming. We've got enough without him."

"Sure," Jacob said. "But that was the best way to get the others. Shan Flannery's a little old for this kind of business, too, but by him coming, and Caleb, and some of the others in town, they got their people to come." Jacob swung his glance away from Jess and probed the near-distance with it. "They're out there—those devils. I rode as far as the knoll yonder after supper. I could feel it."

"We're prepared," Jess said stolidly. "We're doing the best we can."

They rode in silence for a while. Several men emerged out of the night, and one was Caleb Mellon's foreman, Lew Dollarhide, who nodded to Jess and spoke to Jacob.

"Outriders're holding a ten-foot interval, Mr. Harter, on the west side o' the wagons full down the side, like you said, but we'll have to pull in closer when we cross the ridge up ahead. There's a thick brush patch on the yonder side of it."

Jess spoke first. "Don't pull in closer, mister. Go out around the brush."

Dollarhide's squinted eyes shifted to Jess' face. "An' if there's Indians in the brush?"

"That's why you ought to be on the far side. If there's Indians in the brush you'll be behind them and we'll be in front of them."

Jacob listened, then lifted his head and bobbed it. "That's right, Lew. Strategy, boy." Jacob picked up his reins and watched Dollarhide lope back out into the milky night. "I'll tell the men along our east side, Jess."

They grunted their way over the first landswell, and Dollarhide's riders were lost far out in the shadows.

54

There wasn't a man-sound at all as they ground steadily forward.

But the brush held no ambushers.

When Jacob came back he had Caleb Mellon with him. Elizabeth's father grinned at Jess. "Decided to come along at the last minute."

Jess nodded without speaking and looked at Jacob. "I'm going over the grapevine. I'll wait for you up there."

The grapevine was a long, crooked ridge that ran like a broken backbone, east and west mostly, a mile or two ahead of the wagon train's present location. It was known as the area where the hostiles usually kept scouts during the daylight hours. From its windswept, barren eminence, Clybourne could be seen in the southerly distances. Northward, on the far side of the grapevine, lay the roadway, the vast plain that ran all the way to Ten-Mile, and the Indian high country.

He rode at a jog until the clanking, bumping sound of the wagon train was stilled; then he slowed to a walk, unbooted his saddle-gun, lay it athwart his lap and rode with his right fist closed around the gun, his left hand trailing the thin ribbons of reins.

He stayed well in the open, away from the scraggly trees and little bunches of sage and buckbrush that occasionally cast sturdy shadows on the dead-grass prairie. His mind was absorbed by what he was doing. There was danger in the night—he knew that—but there was no peril any closer than the nearest shadows, and he kept them as far away as he could.

When his horse's head went lower and the animal's hooves dug deeper into the rising ground of the grapevine swell, he slowed a little, then stopped. Listening, he didn't expect to hear anything, nor did he.

After a long wait, motionless, alternately watching his horse's ears and straining his own for the least sound, he caught the down-wind whisper of chain-harness and wagons. He swung down, trailed his reins and walked lightly up toward the skyline of the grapevine's twisted ridge. Beyond it, probably, lay the answer to whether they were going to be attacked or not.

He walked up the gradual slope until just his head was above the skyline. There he stopped, holding his carbine at the ready, his palms sweaty and his body erect. The cooling scent of the earth came over the ridge, and as far down the north side as he could see, there was nothing.

He swung forward again and moved up a little farther toward the skyline. That way he had a good view of the surrounding country. Then he saw it. Far off, possibly three miles, the little glowing eyes of campfires—lanterns of the night, the Indians called them—the fires of a big war party. He let his breath out, moved still closer to the skyline and squatted, his rifle held beside him, upright.

His horse threw up its head and twisted for a look backwards. Jess walked down to it, grasped the mane and horn and threw his leg over the cantle. Reining around, he rode toward the sound of a rider coming. It was Jacob, head up and eyes shifting alertly.

"See anything?"

"Yes, their camp's up ahead. Looks like maybe three miles or so." He led the way up the hill, and they sat in silence side by side, studying the little random lights of the Indian campfires. Jacob's breath rattled in his throat.

"Lots of them."

Jess didn't reply.

"Let's go back and pass the word," Jacob said.

56

CHAPTER IV

JACOB RODE ON THE LEFT SIDE, JESS ON THE RIGHT. Wherever they found an outrider they told what they had seen, and rode on. Near the bobbing shadows around the big, ungainly-looking Conestoga, Jess came across Caleb Mellon.

"They're up by Ten-Mile. You'll see their campfires when we cross the grapevine."

"Many?"

"Enough," Jess said.

Elizabeth's father drew the reins through his fist and threw a look northward. "See lights from Ten-Mile yet?"

"No."

Mellon's face, long and solemn, looked sickly grey in the pale light. Then, lowering his voice, he said: "If there *are* any lights up there."

Jess didn't speak. He rode on around the immigrant wagon, looking at it. Outwardly it was another prairie schooner. Perhaps a freighter would notice the extra teams ahead of it, but Indians wouldn't. They wouldn't care if they saw them. Coming around the wagon, he saw the closed ranks of the rear guard and went over to them. They were townsmen. Some he knew he'd seen before, but most were strangers.

"Looks like Indian campfires over the grapevine," he told the burly, bearded, villainous-looking man nearest him. "A lot of them."

The man swore grandly and leaned from his saddle to pass the word along; then he straightened up and squinted at Jess. "How about the fort; still too far off to see?"

57

"Yes." Jess looked into the triangles. The mules and horses being carried along within it had adjusted themselves. Most were grazing as they went. All seemed content.

The bearded man erupted tobacco juice before he spoke again.

"The loose stock act like they been doin' that all their lives."

"Pretty placid now," Jess agreed. "I hope they stay that way."

He rode on around the wagons and up the east side. Jacob met him two thirds of the way down the line. He wheeled and started forward with Jess.

"That woke them up."

"I suppose. Jacob, it makes me a little uneasy. The Indians have no scouts out."

Jacob fluffed his beard from underneath. "They do that now and then, you know. Sometimes you can't get within a mile of an Indian. Next day you could walk up and shoot him out of his britches."

"But not now. Not with a siege and a war going on."

Jacob looked at the grapevine's sere side as the foremost wagons began toiling up it. "You can't ever tell, Jess. Maybe they're making strong-heart medicine."

"I thought that. Getting ready for a big assault on Ten-Mile."

Jacob's gaze was sardonic and speculative. In a very soft voice he said, "Jess, don't tell me you believe that."

"Believe?" Jess asked, looking around. "Believe what?"

"That Ten-Mile's still holding out."

It was like being kicked in the stomach by a mule. Jess let his wind out and drew it back again. "I hadn't thought about it, Jacob—really. Just figured it was, naturally."

"I hope you're right," Jacob said. "But I've got a feeling, Jess."

"Better keep it to yourself."

"Oh, I am. Just you and Caleb know how I feel."

Jess lifted his reins and rode on up toward the point. He passed all five wagons on the east side of the triangle, and every one of the shadowy outriders. Everything looked as it should. The wagon intervals were tight, the men were alert, the harness animals strong and leaning into their collars.

And if Ten-Mile was vanquished?

He lifted his horse into a lope and closed the short distance between the first wagons and the scout's position in short order. He watched the wagons crest the grapevine's broken-back like a huge flight of earth-bound geese. He knew they were all over when he saw the high-swept, dirty old canvas cover of the Conestoga start down the north side and out onto the prairie. That was the last wagon.

He swung around and started back toward the lead wagons.

Jacob was riding point when he got back. The freighter's face was forbidding-looking, with its beard made dark by the moonwash. "They'll hear us within the hour, Jess. Should've heard us sooner."

"I reckon," Jess said shortly, as though he didn't want to talk right now.

They rode side by side far ahead of the wagons for another half-hour. By then Jess' misgivings were too strong to be ignored. He reined up and sat perfectly motionless, staring at the large cluster of campfires far ahead.

59

"There's something wrong, Jacob. Something badly wrong."

Jacob answered, his hopes low but not altogether dead. "Just no scouts out, maybe."

Jess shook his head. "You know better and so do I."

Jacob reined up, dropped his hands and leaned forward, peering at the lights in the night. For a while he was silent; then he gripped the saddlehorn with both hands and spoke without looking away from the Indian camp up ahead. "It's spooky."

"It's more than that. They'd never let us get this close without trouble. There's something darned strange up there."

"It's awful quiet," Jacob said.

Jess sat lost in thought. He waited until the sound of the train was very close; then he lifted his reins and held them a moment, staring. "Jacob, go down the line and pick out fifteen or twenty men, will you? Have them follow me."

"Where are you going?"

"Up ahead until I can see Ten-Mile. I've got a feeling . . ."

Jacob looked bleak. "You won't have to get too close."

Almost angrily Jess loped away.

He rode a full twenty minutes in a long, loping gallop; then he hauled down to a stiff-slamming trot, before finally pulling his mount down into a walk. There wasn't a sign of an Indian anywhere. His horse began to act uneasy when they were on the last lap of the Ten-Mile road. He stopped and waited, feeling his scalp shifting under his hat. Riders were making a drumroll reverberation in the ground under him. He could feel it through the seating leather. When they came swirling up he scarcely threw them a look. Gigging his chestnut horse, he tossed his head. They followed.

When a strong scent came up to him it made him lock his jaws until the muscles rippled along the angle of his cheek. All of them smelt it, but none commented as they might have at any other time.

Up ahead was a dark, squatty, ugly outline. There were no lights showing over its rammed-earth and pine-pole walls and stockades. This was Fort Ten-Mile.

"Hold it."

They crowded up behind him. A horse snorted and a rider cursed him. No arrow came—no bullet—nothing. One of the men kneed up to Jess.

"Let's go on. We're no worse off closer in than we are sitting here like tame pigeons."

"No, they must know we're here by now. Can't help but know it. The wagon train's sounds would carry to their camp. It might be an ambush."

The man said, "Yeah, and it might just as well be; there's no one left inside Ten-Mile."

Jess heard without heeding. Up ahead the ghostly outline, eerie in the pale, milky light, was deathly silent. Jess was puzzled. There was something unreal, uncanny, about the brooding shadow facing westward on the far rise. It bulked large and dark. The only sound that was softly borne to them where they sat in their vacuum was from the distant wagons. Without looking away from the frowning fort up ahead, he spoke to the man beside him.

"Go back and tell Harter to make a big swing with the train. Bring it in facing the fort. Tell him there's no sign of life up here—no lights."

The man rode away at a stiff-legged trot. The sound

of his going was the only thing that broke the hush. Jess swung his glance westward. The Indian fires were burning low, off to his left. He estimated them to be half or three quarters of a mile away, but the night was glass-clear; they might be farther. The wagon sounds were closer. He looked at the men with him and read the same dread in their expressions that he felt.

"Come on."

They followed him at a flat-footed walk, making a huge circle around behind Fort Ten-Mile. The smell of dead things was overpowering as they got closer.

When he went wide behind the fort, around the little ledge where the silence was thickest, the smell wasn't so bad. They came across their first dead horse there.

Tightening his encirclement a little, Jess continued on around the place, north, then westerly. There, the signs of battle were thicker. Indian accoutrements—lances, an occasional carbine, medicine-shields, even blood-stiff blankets and bows, war-bonnets and more dead horses, grotesque-looking with their vividly painted symbols.

Jess stopped beside a big grey horse with eagle feathers braided into its mane and foretop. He swung down and hooked his booted toe under the animal's foreleg, pushed, then withdrew his foot. The horse was stiff. He had been dead quite some time. On its right shoulder was the blood-red imprint of an open hand. Every frontiersman knew the sign of the Bloody Custer—the most fearful symbol of them all. It meant that the warrior who rode a horse so marked had sworn to triumph on his war trail or perish.

He raised his head and listened. The train was making its wide curve out on the flat before Fort Ten-Mile's ledge. He swung up and flagged the riders after him, riding in a loose lope down toward the train.

When he met Jacob the wagon master had a bristling corps of big-eyed, silent men around him.

"What is it, Jess? Where are they?"

"I don't know. Ten-Mile's been battling hard. That's all I can say right now. Let me take those men you have and ride up there."

Jacob nodded. Jess' gaze flickered over the riders. Caleb Mellon was among them. There were others he recognized vaguely as he wheeled his horse and started toward the fort. Softly, he heard Jacob call for the train to halt.

The men riding with him were stiff silhouettes with set, granite faces. Off to the north a wolf let off his baleful howl, and behind Jess a man swore edgily.

The gate loomed up. Jess stared at it. If this was an ambush it would explode in their faces when they were close enough for killing accuracy. There was no other way. He lifted the Dragoon pistol from its holster and held it in his hand and never slackened pace.

When they were all close enough to the fort to see it clearly, the gaping hole where the gate had been was visible. A ripple of understanding went through the horsemen behind him.

With a dry mouth, Jess rode into the breached fort. The sound of horses' hooves jolting across the dusty earth of the assembly area set up ghostly echoes in the moonlit night.

There were dark, flat objects lying at random as though cast with a giant's scorn among the gutted ruin inside Fort Ten-Mile. Jess stopped and looked. The night shadowed a lot of it but too much was painfully, starkly clear to every man in the relief column.

Too late.

He dismounted stiffly and watched the riders follow

his example. Someone brushed against his elbow, and he turned. It was Caleb Mellon. The buggy maker's face was slack-muscled, sagging. He didn't say a word.

The little hutments that had been built against the walls inside the fort were lonely and tragic-looking. Doors had been torn off or beaten in. Attempts to fire the place hadn't been successful, but there was enough char to indicate it had been tried. Bodies were everywhere, and they weren't all soldiers. Women, too, had died in the flaming, screaming holocaust.

Jess swung toward Elizabeth's father. "I'm going back. You pick who you want—search the place for survivors." He swung up into the saddle, then thoughtfully bent forward toward Mellon. "There used to be a mint bed behind the O. D. hut. Rub it into your handkerchiefs and tie them over your faces. It'll help overcome the smell."

Jacob had corralled the wagons with the loose stock inside. He was with a big body of men between the fort and the train when Jess rode up to him.

"We're too late, Jacob. Looks like it's been all over with Ten-Mile for over two days."

Jacob nodded and repressed a shudder. "I figured. Too quiet, Jess."

"Where are you going now?" Jess asked.

"To the fort."

"Let the others go. Take a little ride with me."

Jacob's gaze remained unmoving for a moment; then he nodded his head and looked at the men with him. "Go ahead."

Jess looked at the men. "It might help," he said, "if you took some picks and shovels up there."

He and Jacob rode northwest, side by side. When Ten-Mile was a short distance behind them, they swung

64

south and made for a little hummock. From the rim they could see the glow from campfires that was the Indian encampment. Jess' perplexity turned to something more nearly akin to a sinking fear. With less caution than he would ordinarily have shown, he plunged down off the hillock with Jacob Harter following.

"Jess . . ."

"There won't be any," Jess said cryptically. "If they'd had scouts out we wouldn't have gotten this far." He rode a hundred feet before he spoke again. "There wasn't an ambush set up at the fort either. That means they've left."

"Loaded and gone home," Jacob said. "There might be a few left around."

Jess didn't speak. He rode boldly toward the foremost little fire. Its ashes were akin to the alkali taste in his mouth. There wasn't an Indian anywhere.

"Let's go back," Jess said.

They rode in silence. Back inside the fort men were busy in the chilling moonlight digging graves. Caleb Mellon came up with a mint-scented handkerchief over the lower part of his face. "We can't drink the water here," he said. "We found a dead horse in it."

Jacob was struck dumb by the carnage. Jess turned away from him, toward Elizabeth's father. "Any dead Indians?"

"Not a one."

Jacob tugged his eyes away from the grisly work going on around them. "They take away their dead."

"I know that," Jess said shortly. "What I'm trying to figure out is how long ago they did this—how long they've been gone. If it was daylight we could read the sign on the ground." He gave a hollow laugh. "We were so clever we outsmarted ourselves."

Mellon looked at them both over the edge of his mask. "Not a survivor and I'd say, from the looks of the looted hutments, they must have had at least a full day's run of the fort. What they didn't take they ruined." He coughed behind the handkerchief. "That would put the fall of the fort day before yesterday. They spent one day, at least, looting, stripping the dead—all the rest of it."

Jess nodded in silence.

The burial parties were hard pressed. Aside from the sun-packed flintiness of the ground, it had also been hammered granite-hard by the ceaseless pounding of many hooves.

Softly, Caleb Mellon said: "There's still a little hoarded food in the mess-hall and the kitchen. The Indians broke up what they didn't want. They weren't starved out then. How was it done?"

"Any breaks in the walls?" Jacob asked. "Ladders? Tunnels?"

"Nothing that we could find." Mellon was looking at Jess. "It's a mystery."

"It probably always will be," Jess said, turning away.

The mystery was more than just the breaching of Fort Ten-Mile and the ensuing fight that had ended in overwhelming defeat and massacre of the vanquished. It haunted him.

Walking out through the open gate into the pale gloom beyond, he was conscious of his surroundings, acutely so, but only as the source of something that was nagging him: the reason for the empty Sioux encampment; the answer to the riddle of how Ten-Mile had been taken.

"Jess."

He turned. It was Caleb Mellon, and he was holding

66

something limp and white in his hand. "I don't know whether this is the appropriate time to hand you this or not."

"What is it?"

"Just before I left the house Elizabeth gave it to me to give to you."

Jess took the paper, looked at it in a troubled way, then nodded at Caleb. The older man turned and walked back into the fort.

Staring at the note, Jess held it without making any move to open it. He thrust the envelope into his jacket pocket and walked swiftly back inside where his horse was. He was in the act of mounting when Jacob Harter, with a minted handkerchief and sick-looking eyes, stopped beside him.

"Where are you going?"

"To look for tracks—read the sign. There's a reason for this silence. I'm going to find it."

"Wait," Jacob said. "I'll go too."

Caleb Mellon and Shan Flannery were left in charge, along with the young lieutenant, whose face was tinted a ghastly green. Jacob removed his mask when they were a hundred yards west of the fort, heading up toward the sullen little splotches of dying coals.

Circling farther out, afoot also, Jacob Harter was humped over like an unkempt gnome: a caricature of a broad, squatty man, in the murky predawn.

"Here, Jess; here's where they gathered before they struck out."

Jess went over. The sign was wide and clear. Many horses; much milling of riders. Here the hostiles had talked before they'd left. He went slowly westward until the tracks showed a wide span between hoof-marks.

67

"They went due west, Jacob. Let's follow them for a way."

They rode for fully an hour; then the tracks swung south as abruptly as though there had been a marked road there. Jacob hauled up with a frowning expression and a ragged curse. He scowled into the distance, sat a moment, then rode shufflingly, slowly, back to where Jess had dismounted and was standing erect and stiff-looking.

"What's the matter? Hear something?"

Without answering Jess turned, toed into the stirrup and sprang up. "No," he said, and that was all.

Jacob peered at him, kneeing his horse closer. "What is it, Jess?"

"I've got to be wrong. I've got to be!"

That was all he'd say until they were loping into the gate of Fort Ten-Mile. He flung down off his horse and grabbed a soldier with a violent grip.

"Where's Mellon?"

Startled, perspiring and ill-looking, the trooper waved his right hand vaguely. "Over there, over by the horse sheds."

"Come on, Jacob."

Mellon was working with his coat off. His shirt was dark and sticky with perspiration. At Jess' spur-rattle he looked up quickly, inquiringly, and drew himself upright. "You find them? What is it?"

"Jacob and I're going to take a ride. I've got a hunch, Caleb. If I'm wrong we'll be back shortly. If I'm right— Jacob'll be back."

"All right," Mellon said, "what did you find?"

"Tracks," Jess said. "Come on, Jacob."

Harter hadn't dismounted. He and Caleb exchanged worried looks. Jacob lifted his shoulders and let them fall, wheeled his horse and spurred out behind Jess.

They rode due south following the trail the wagon train had covered only a short time before. Their horses, sensing the homing direction, ran with a strong, good will. Jacob's head swung from side to side constantly.

Sweeping up the north side of the grapevine, Jess slammed his horse into a dirt-flinging slide. Jacob, caught unprepared, went part way down the hill before he stopped. Indignantly he swung his head, glared up at Jess who was sitting perfectly motionless, head up and body still; a statue.

Then Jacob heard it, too. Gunfire! Puzzled, he turned and looked south. Jess' voice broke into his quandary.

"Come up here; you can see it." There was something bleak and brittle in the words.

Jacob rode back up the hill and twisted, following Jess' line of sight. He let out a gust of breath and a terrible blasphemy. Jess spoke to him without taking his eyes off the distant sight of Clybourne under attack, with tongues of flame billowing skyward, limning scenes they could only imagine.

"I was right. Go back and get the others. Every mule that will carry a man—every horse—put two on them. Kill the animals if you have to, Jacob, but bring them all, and hurry!"

He lifted his big chestnut horse with the spurs and sent him plunging down the grade without glancing at Harter. The wagon-master reacted slowly, with a kind of snow-balling momentum of emotion. When he swerved his horse and leaned forward, he hooked the animal mercilessly and sent it into a lunging, belly-down run back toward the fort.

Jess rode hard until he felt his horse falter. He slowed then, with the need for speed mocking him. If he could ride through the cordon of attacking Indians, what good would it do?

When he dropped down to a walk, he could smell the burning buildings and see the small silhouettes of careening warriors assaulting the north end of Clybourne. Seeking shelter, he found the brush patch Mellon's foreman had worried about on the outward trip. He rode into it and sat there, helpless, watching.

Two things were in the favor of the townsmen. Jess had discovered the purpose of the Indians' ruse before the town had been under attack very long. That, and the fact that the hostiles had held off hitting Clybourne until the first dawn-light came. He surmised the fires had been started by warriors who sneaked in close enough to let off fire arrows, just ahead of the main attack. That Clybourne had been paralyzed by the suddenness, the unexpectedness, he could imagine, but that those who hadn't gone out with the wagon train were putting up a fierce resistance, he knew from listening to the steady, vicious hammering of gunshots.

Warrior cries came faintly to him in the brush patch. It looked as though the Indians had planned on a lightning attack of terrible ferocity, probably planning to overwhelm Clybourne as they had Fort Ten-Mile, then turn upon the wagon train. Three smashing victories within forty-eight hours. It would give the Sioux War an impetus nothing else could. Indians would flock to the red man's banner from all over the West.

He turned sideways and strained for the sound of the relief column from Ten-Mile. There was only the soughing of a soft, low breeze that hurried stealthily through the dead grass.

Elizabeth was down there.

His hands were damp and crabbed-feeling, one

holding his reins, the other his pistol.

While he waited, watching the battle from his little brushy knoll, he noted that the Indians were attacking the town in their customary encircling way but that the main brunt of the attacking waves was thrown against the north and south entrances of Clybourne.

Within Clybourne itself it was impossible to make out the people. The smoke was thick and billowing, but mainly his view of the town was blocked by the dust and furor created by the hordes of red horsemen.

He turned repeatedly and bent, straining to catch the sound of riders even though he knew it would take time for them to cover the distance. Out of the north there was only the deep silence with its echoes of the battle south of him.

The daylight lengthened; his position wasn't too secure, for occasional parties of wounded went straggling northwest. None came due north, near him, but at any moment some might. He shifted his seat many times and watched the fury of the battle with a choked feeling.

Just before the sun began inching over the horizon he heard horses coming behind him. It was a throbbing thunder telegraphed far ahead under the hardpan. Many horses and many men.

The first one he recognized was Dollarhide, Mellon's foreman. The second one was a lanky rider with a twisted, red, dirt-smudged face and bulging eyes, straining hard to see ahead, his mouth hanging agape. The third man to crest the landswell was Caleb Mellon. That was when Jess reined out of the brush and flagged his arm at the stampeding riders.

They jarred to a swirling halt around him. Horses bore double; one man in the saddle, another behind the cantle. Mules that had never carried a man before were carrying at least one now, and most of them had running

71

W's or hastily made war bridles under their upper lips to keep their heads up and prevent their bucking off the bareback riders.

"Let's go!" Mellon roared.

Jess yelled, "Wait!" He saw Mellon's face up close. It was drained of color. His lips were blue and turned in upon one another. His shaggy, leonine head was held high in defiance, like a strong-heart Sioux buck.

"Jacob?"

"Here."

"They're concentrating around the north and south ends of town. Hadn't we better split up and hit them both places?"

Before Jacob could answer the young lieutenant urged a lathered horse forward. "No!" he said flatly. "Don't split up! Stay together. They outnumber us. Split up, they'll ride over the top of us."

Jacob's eyes were red as though stung with sharp particles in the air during his race against time. "That's right, Jess," he said. "If we hit 'em down there, the ones from the south'll come up to get into the fight anyway."

Mellon cried out a curse. "Don't talk—ride!" He swung his horse and hung in the spurs. The beast, jaded and wringing wet, switched his tail furiously, protestingly, then fled down the new day toward Clybourne.

"HOPPO!"

It rang from a hundred throats as the impatient men threw their mounts into a dead run behind Caleb Mellon. Over the quivering roll of horses running on a loose rein, Jess' own cry sounded flatly.

"HOKA-HAY!" (Charge, in Sioux.)

They charged.

CHAPTER V

THERE WAS LITTLE ORGANIZATION TO THE CHARGE. Men went according to the speed of their horses. They were strung out in a long line with a skeleton rank behind where the lagging animals came along under the whips, spurs and the imprecations and coaxings of their riders.

Jess checked his horse, the freshest of the entire cavalcade. He rode beside Jacob Harter, who was astride a good sorrel mare. For Jess, the long, agonizing wait had been a prelude to the cold calm that now possessed him. He was almost detached in his scrutiny of the men flowing in a huge, inward curving line on both sides of him. It was a ludicrous sight in one way, a pathetic sight in another way, but any way he looked at it, two men bouncing along on one flap-eared mule was a grim spectacle. Some had their guns up already, although the range was still too great.

When they swept past the first gathering of Indians it was in the face of a mangled cry of astonishment. Jess fired twice at a tall buck and missed him both times. Turning in the saddle for a third shot as he swept past, he saw the Indian spun drunkenly by the explosion of a .45-70 in the hands of a white-faced youth.

The Indians sent up wild screams of warning to their attacking companions closer to town. Jess threw a fast look at Caleb Mellon. The buggy maker's horse was floundering badly. While Jess watched the beast collapsed slowly, leaving the rider standing astride him.

Jacob was yelling something and drawing his horse to a stiff-legged stop. Jess couldn't understand the words, but several other of the cooler heads took up Jacob's

73

cry. Men began to dismount on the fly. Some flung their reins away and knelt almost as soon as their feet touched the ground. The firing became deafening; the confusion worse. The wounded and resting Indians, close, were scrambling for their horses or, lacking those, were trying to flee. A withering volley of gunfire ripped into them.

Jess slapped his big chestnut horse across the nose with his hat. The animal threw his head sideways, dragging the reins, turned and galloped back the way he had come. Better to risk his loss to some dismounted Sioux buck than to have him killed where he was. The Indians invariably shot horses first.

A man fell against him, sideways. He fought for his balance and turned after he'd gotten it. It was a soldier. He had a third eye above the other two.

The mounted bucks down by the northern approaches to Clybourne were coming back in a shrieking charge. Jess' heart missed a beat. Behind them were other warriors streaming up from the plain on both sides of the town. There were more fighting Indians than he'd ever seen in one place before.

A quavering cry went up from the embattled Clybourneites behind the ranks of Sioux and Northern Cheyenne warriors. Jess heard it without drawing much encouragement from it. Jacob Harter tugged at his sleeve and bellowed into his ear.

"Get down! Kneel down! Hold your fire until you can't miss!"

Jess knelt, twisting his head. The exposed townsmen were copying the little clutch of soldiers, who were kneeling, rifles up, steady and waiting. The wall of Indians swept through the confusion and wreckage of their fellows, who had absorbed the first shattering blast

74

from the relieving column, and kept right on coming. The youth next to Jess jumped up and let out a shrill scream. Jess grabbed his leg and pulled viciously. The boy fell, rolled over and lay face down shaking as though with a fever.

The solid wall of gunsmoke all but hid the townsmen when they fired a second after the soldiers had. Those with single-shot carbines and rifles tore frettingly at their breeches to reload. Then men with later models levered up the next bullet and snugged in their guns, held low, and fired. After the second volley the firing became more erratic and less cohesive.

Jess' pistol was empty. He appropriated the Stevens rifle of the boy beside him, tossed his pistol down and tracked a big Sioux with a soldier's coat that was unbuttoned and too tight. He held on him briefly and tugged off the slug. The warrior sagged, grasped sluggishly at his horse's mane, missed and went off sideways. Instantly those behind him swept up and over his body, obscuring it in the dust.

Jacob Harter was swearing in a frenzied way, without coherence. Jess looked at him. He slammed his jaw closed and made a hideous grimace.

"They're still coming. Look—streaming around town from the south entrance. This is a bad spot."

"Not as bad a spot as they're in," Jess bellowed, "if we can hold 'em. Look behind 'em—down by town."

Men were forming afoot down there. True, it was a pathetic scraggly line of boys who hadn't begun to shave and old men whose gnarled fingers clutched hickory-stocked old Hawken and Pennsylvania muskets, but it was a fighting force and it was advancing slowly, steadily, against the rear of the attackers. The Indians had to present their backs to the fire of the villagers, their faces to the murderous volleys of the men who had ridden their horses nearly to death in the race back from devastated Fort Ten-Mile.

Jess emptied the carbine and turned to cast it aside. The boy who owned it was sitting up and using both hands to fire Jess' reloaded pistol. Tears streamed down his face and his mouth worked spasmodically, but he was firing into the face of the Indians.

"Here," Jess yelled, "load the thing." He took back his hand-gun and swung around in one long movement.

The Indians' losses were sickening but they still tried to ride, claw or fight their way toward the uneven line of white men. Horses were fleeing with heads high, tails straight out. Others were standing apart, heads down, dying. The carnage was terrible, and when Jess was certain the reformed line of warriors would overwhelm them, the Indians broke and fled every whichway. They streamed out around the embattled relief column and turned to pour in a furious flanking fire. Jess and Jacob Harter were in the middle of the ragged line; too far away to fire effectively. Jess let his gun hand drop slowly, turning as he did so to watch the hostiles race away, still screaming and firing useless shots. Beside him, Jacob drew in a rattling breath that caught in his throat. He made a wet, gravelly sound and spat.

"I could be sick, Jess."

Jess looked at him. His hat was gone and one pants leg dripped blood below the knee. "Shock, Jacob. You're hit."

"The devil I am," Jacob said, looking down, following the trajectory of Jess' glance. "I am! I sure am!" Without another word Jacob dropped down lower, pushed his wounded leg out in front of him and, ignoring the dying furor, calmly tugged up his britches

76

leg and peered at the long, diagonal slash in his calf where a ricochetting bullet had gouged him.

Jess got up and flexed his legs. Others were moving among their companions. Down the line was Caleb Mellon with his hand stuffed inside his shirt. He looked dazed where before he had looked grim and raging. Jess walked down to him. Closer he saw the soggy, scarlet red of Mellon's shirt-front. His heart sank.

"Gut-shot?"

"No," Mellon said thickly. "Two fingers gone."

Jess breathed again. "Sit down. Standing up won't help it any."

"I wrapped it up. I've got to—"

Mellon fainted.

Jess felt helpless for a moment; then he knelt and gingerly withdrew the bleeding hand. The finger stumps were gushing. With a curse he made a piece of Mellon's sleeve into a cloth rope and lashed it brutally tight around the man's wrist.

"Is he dead?"

Jess looked up. It was Mellon's buggy works foreman, Lew Dollarhide. He shook his head. "No, but he could have been. He wrapped up the hand and didn't tie off the blood supply." Arising, Jess said, "You take care of him, will you? I'll go down to town and get some buggies to fetch the wounded."

"How about the Indians; won't they come back?"

Jess said, "The Indians have had enough."

He struck out for Clybourne.

The people from town were breaking up into two groups: those who had brothers, fathers, sons, among the relief column; and those who were eager to take up guns and trophies from the dead Indians. Both groups split up and went around him. Some called out, others nodded, a few smiled even, but mostly the townsmen were as frozen-faced, as uncompromising-looking as Jess himself was.

In Clybourne a bucket brigade was squelching the last of the fires. A red-faced man soaked with perspiration swung with a curse as Jess came up.

"She's done. She's plumb done and put out. Hope it never happens like that again! Firemen had to fight fire and duck bullets all through the cussed fight and dassn't stop tossing water long enough to take a crack at the Injuns."

"How were your casualties?"

The man mopped at his forehead and threw out the same arm, pointing. "I don't know. Seen 'em takin' folks into Flannery's store, but haven't been around there myself."

"Thanks."

He went first to the Mellons' place. There was no one there, nor had he expected there to be. Next he went to Flannery's.

Inside were most of the women of Clybourne. There were blood-stained sheets split into bandages and the injured in long, staggered lines on the floor between the counters. It was an unnerving sight when he looked at the faces—blank, pale, blue-lipped, eyes closed.

Off to one side squatted the ambulatory wounded. There were old men and too young boys. Everywhere he looked he saw blood: on the floor, on the counter where a doctor worked with streaked forearms and a sunken pair of eyes, on the aprons and dresses of the women.

He caught an elderly woman as she went by. A wavy strand of brown-grey hair hung jauntily over her forehead. While she listened to Jess' question, she thrust out her lower lip and blew upward. The hair flipped up into place.

78

"Is Miss Mellon around, ma'am? Have you seen her?"

Her eyes were steely grey and deep-looking. She seemed to hang over her answer for a moment, looking at him. "Did you come with the wagon train?"

"Well, the men from the train came back, but the wagons're still at Ten-Mile."

"Did you bring back the people with you?"

He looked directly at her. "Have you seen Miss Mellon?"

Her mouth moved a little and her eyes got a shiny look. "I had a son in Ten-Mile," she said. "Did you bring them back?"

"No'm. We buried most of them there."

"No, I haven't seen Miss Mellon." She walked away too quickly for Jess to thank her. His heart was like lead.

"Jess."

It was Tarney Wilkins, one of Jacob Harter's teamsters. He'd stayed behind because of a recent rattlesnake bite. Jess dropped down beside his pallet. "Bad, Tarney?"

"If the snake couldn't do it, I don't allow this will."

"Where is it?"

"Belly. How was they at Ten-Mile?"

"The doctor fixed you yet?"

Wilkins' eyes lost their forced pleasantness and grew very still. "Jess, you wouldn't beat around the bush, would you?"

"No, Tarney, I guess not. They were wiped out."

"Amen," Tarney Wilkins said after a space. "Amen. There was an old army wagoneer up there—friend of mine—biggest liar in the West . . ."

"Tarney, where's Elizabeth Mellon?"

79

But Tarney Wilkins' head was averted and the bulge of his jaw showed how hard he was clamping his teeth.

Jess got up and looked out over the rows of injured people. He was going to move when Harter's teamster spoke.

"Jess?"

"Yes?"

"Buried 'em up there?"

"There's a lot we didn't get to, Tarney. I smelt this buffalo trick they pulled and came back here hell-for-leather."

"Maybe I could go up later."

"Sure you can, old-timer. They died game."

Wilkins' eyes were cloudy. "Miz' Mellon, you asked about. She's gone, Jess. When they first hit us we forted up. You boys didn't leave us near enough men to hold the town. We had women an' kids and old grandpaws with squirrel guns out there."

"What do you mean—gone—Tarney?"

"I'm telling you. We had to send for help and dassn't spare a man strong enough to ride nor a boy big enough to hold up a gun. She went."

"For help?" Jess said blankly. "Where?"

"Camp Lincoln, Jess."

Tarney Wilkins' glance was still and soft. He understood. Jess was rooted, gazing down at the wounded man. When his voice came out it was just above a whisper, and low.

"Camp Lincoln. Tarney, that's . . ."

"I know, I know. Through Sioux country. What else could we do, boy? Put yourself in our fix. We dassn't spare a man. There's no other help within three days' hard riding. Jess, none of us wanted her to try it, but someone had to."

80

Jess said, "Thanks, Tarney. Get well fast. We'll need you as soon as things get back to normal. S'long."

He wound his way among the people without seeing any of them. Camp Lincoln! Sixty miles northwest—right through the heart of the hostiles' country. Those two words shredded his hope and made him feel defeated, and he hurt deep inside where it wouldn't ever heal.

The sun was blinding as it glanced off the dust particles in the air. He went through it, and the dust, and the noisy bedlam of Clybourne, toward the livery barn. He never got to his destination. Lew Dollarhide, astride a big Indian horse with gaudy symbols painted on it and a forlorn eagle feather dangling from its foretop, came plodding down the road with a string of led horses.

"Jess! Oh, Jess! I got your chestnut here."

He freed his horse from the tangled skein of reins and lead ropes, swung up and waved his thanks to Dollarhide, spun around and headed north out of Clybourne.

The battlefield was filled with people. Already two big wagons were gathering the dead Indians like cordwood. Buggies and smaller wagons were going out too, and coming back from the line where the Fort Ten-Mile relief party had made its stand. The wounded lay stoically through the jolting ride. As he passed some of the improvised ambulances he glanced down into them.

Jacob Harter was limping, leading two big mules with arrow shafts sticking in them, one in the shoulder, one in the hip. He stopped when he saw Jess coming.

"Where you going: back to Ten-Mile?"

"No," Jess said tiredly. "Up into the trees a way, then to sleep until dark."

Harter looked nonplussed. "What the blazes for?"

81

"Elizabeth Mellon rode for Camp Lincoln and help. Going after her."

"She WHAT!"

"They couldn't spare a man for the job."

Harter wagged his head disbelievingly. "Who told you that, anyway?"

"Tarney Wilkins. He's wounded, lying over at Flannery's store."

A glance at Jacob Harter's dumbfounded expression was all Jess had, and that fleetingly. He reined out around the injured mules and kept on going.

The heat was bad, but there was relief of a kind in getting away from the twin tragedies that would hold Clybourne in the grip of grief for a long time. Besides, he wanted to be alone.

Using every screen of cover he could find without riding closer than gunshot to any of them, he wound his way northwest. When the sun had burned the sky a spotless, faded blue, he was nearing the first shaggy outthrust of forest, and by the time it had dropped a little past the meridian, he was in among the pines and firs.

The fragrance was pleasant. The shade was even more welcome than the smell. He left his horse where the underbrush was the thickest and scouted afoot. To be doubly sure no Indians had preceded him into the forest's fringe, he made a huge circle. There were no tracks; no crushed pine needles oozing oil. He slugged his way up the side-hill a mile, found a little clearing and squatted on the high side of it.

Through the trees was the brassy plain. Clybourne was an infinitesimal speck. Where the fight had been that morning he couldn't discern anything, even though he knew men were busy down there. He went back down to his horse and burrowed into the brush, used his hat for a pillow, and slept. It was a deep, exhausted slumber, untroubled and undisturbed. When he awoke hours later the stars were overhead, winking in a brittle way. He lay without moving, without thinking.

It would be hopeless to try and track her down now. Perhaps, after he was far enough overland in Sioux country, he might cut her sign. She'd make a bee-line for Camp Lincoln. The fact that she rode a shod horse would help, but not a whole lot. After the Ten-Mile defeat a lot of warriors would be riding trooper horses. They would also be shod.

He got up and stretched, mounted the chestnut horse and rode northwest. The necessity for riding at night negated the usefulness of horse tracks—at least this first night. There would be Indians watching the town and Ten-Mile like hawks. He'd have to forego daylight until he was far across Indian country to risk moving during the light hours.

If he picked up her tracks up by Lincoln—fine. He'd know they were hers easily enough; no hostiles rode within a day's ride of the army camp. Where the danger lay was between Camp Lincoln and the heart of the hostiles' country.

The forest was as gloomy and unfriendly at night as it was fragrant and pleasant during the day. He let the chestnut horse pretty much pick his own way.

Just before dawn he rode out of the trees and found himself at the edge of an immense meadow. He reined up and sat there, head up. There wasn't a sound, but something within him jangled a warning. Irritated at the delay, he nevertheless swung down, loosened the saddle and hung the bridle on the horn. Buckling on the figure-eight hobbles, he let his horse graze, after tugging out his carbine.

The craving for a cigarette plagued him, although he rarely smoked. Working his way back among the trees, he dropped down at the base of a lightning-struck fir, cradled the carbine and threw impatient glances eastward. A cougar screamed. His horse threw up its head and snorted softly. After that the silence and the minutes trooped past with feet of lead. There was nothing to give him an idea of the passage of time; no high-curving sun or lengthening shadows. His impatience grew until the first splinter of weak color wedged itself between the horizon and the sky.

He went out, caught his horse, led him back out of the meadow grass and in among the trees. After he bridled him and tightened the cincha, he left him tied. He took his carbine and walked carefully forward.

At the edge of the forest he stayed deep in the shadows and studied the big meadow as the light grew. Far out on it was an irregular dark blotch. He squatted down, watching. When it was bright enough, he grunted softly to himself. Indians.

They either had a lot of wounded with them or they had been too exhausted to keep on going. In their numbers was their strength, though, for there were several hundred anyway, judging from the size of the horse herd. He stood up, again flexed his legs and went back to his horse. Booting the carbine, he mounted and struck out just within the tree fringe, due west.

That was his first test. He had sensed the danger in time and avoided it.

His second worry came upon him unexpectedly. Watching ahead and on both sides as he rode, there was nothing to alarm him until he stopped in a tiny wind-swept clearing and threw a long, searching gaze all around. Then he saw them—seven bucks astride and two afoot who trotted ahead, twisting and turning,

84

following his tracks, far behind.

He sat there watching, thinking there was only one direction to go now—ahead. The knowledge that he was being tracked made him more alert and wary.

He urged his horse finally when he came to the end of the forest's western sweep. Beyond lay the shimmering land. It was like being naked, riding out there after the protection of the trees. He puckered his eyes against the glare and rode northward, eyes never still and his right hand hanging ready beside the Dragoon pistol.

Of sign there was plenty. All barefoot horses, though. That worried him until he figured he was far enough ahead of the pursuit; then he swung west again and kept going. Camp Lincoln was northward. If Elizabeth was riding straight for the place, he'd eventually cut her sign—providing she'd gotten this far.

Twice he saw Indians. Once it was the dogged men behind him breaking out of the forest. They were small in the hazy distance. The second time was when several travois plodded past, having come around the forest. There would be wounded men on the hide slings made fast to the dual poles of the travois. He watched without sympathy for the men so hauled.

It occurred to him that the outline of his hat would tell any Indian at a distance he was a white man. He took it off and shoved it inside his shirt. Then the sun really began to bother him.

When dusk came he was still plodding westward, watching the ground. If he was caught here—in the heart of the Indian hunting grounds—he wouldn't have a chance. There was no place to hide; nothing to make for if a savage raised the yell. It was open country.

The imprints of many unshod horses showed now. Travois marks, like snakes, went trailing off both northward and westward. He began to have misgivings. The farther he went the surer he was of being discovered. His uneasiness made him ride over the imprints of a shod horse before he reined up, craned his neck and looked back.

There was no mistaking them. He raised his glance and fixed it in the true direction of the army post, then wheeled and began to follow the marks. If he was wrong . . .

The pursuing warriors must have seen him, or at least surmised that the little speck moving several miles ahead of them was their prey. The last time Jess looked back at them they were pushing their horses hard after him, despite the crushing heat. He smiled crookedly. Let them come; let them run those horses a full two miles in this heat. If the animals didn't give out, they'd die from the exertion.

After that he ignored his enemies, concentrated on the shod-horse tracks and boosted his chestnut into a loose-jointed, kidney-slamming trot. Right or wrong, he couldn't risk any more delay in getting to Camp Lincoln.

The land shimmered, a pale haze hung over it, and the color of his horse got darker, more bronzed-looking and shiny. He held to the trot, as uncomfortable as it was, knowing it was the fastest gait he dared take out of the animal. Heat stroke now would be fatal.

Far ahead and to his right there was a dun dust cloud hanging inertly in the air. He surmised that would be over the main band of fighting Indians and kept his eye on it. Twice he saw tiny dots race callously toward the dust banner from farther west. More Sioux or Cheyennes hurrying to catch up with the warrior column. An uneasy feeling prompted him to look down his back-trail again. The seven bucks were still coming, but at a walk now. He lifted his lip in a humorless way. They had pushed their horses too hard. Now, if they caught up to him at all, it would have to be on other animals.

The land began to break up into gradually increasing lifts and falls. There were shallow gullies with gravel at their bottoms from the winter runoff. Scrub-oak clumps and shaggy old junipers, twisted and gnarled, helped to break the glaring monotony of the prairie. Shadows were creeping out on the west sides of trees, rocks, and brush patches. The sun was a red ball hanging low in the west.

Dipping over a rib of gravelly land with only the sound of his horse's shoes making grating sounds, Jess came upon a freshly erected Sioux burial platform. He reined up suddenly, the hair along the back of his neck bristling. He could almost smell Indians. A quick glance showed how freshly the platform had been erected. Atop it was the blanket-swaddled form of a body lying flat, head covered but looking skyward nevertheless. A horse had been tied to one leg of the scaffolding and shot. He lay as though in sleep, his body still wearing the vivid ochre, black, and chalk-white symbols of a fighting man's mount. In his tail was a solitary red feather with a white bar across its lower extremity and a white dot below the bar. Hidatsa Sioux.

Swinging wide around the dead man and his horse, Jess picked up the shod-horse tracks again, farther westward, and plodded after them. From time to time he raised his eyes to the dust cloud far ahead and off to the left. It was moving as slowly as he was, cutting diagonally across his route. His mouth was dry with foreboding. Unless the rider of the shod horse was an Indian—he or she had better have made the tracks he

87

was following at least five hours ago.

The land became so broken and twisted he was compelled for safety's sake to reconnoiter every hill before he breasted it. The precaution was time-consuming. He fretted at the need for caution but fortunately he heeded it, for in the early dusk he came around a knobby hill where the air was cooler and the trees thicker, and saw a cabin of cottonwood logs hugging a shady corner where a little creek meandered past.

No Indian made that cabin. He rode into a patch of trees quickly and sat there. It could be one of those homestead claims the trespassing whites had made . . . Only it wasn't. The log ends were still pasty-white. It was a freshly built cabin. Indian? No, he knew better than that. Whites? It was unlikely. He shifted his position so he could command a good view of the entire area. Back in the trees where one corner dipped and included a little of the creek was a pole horse-corral. It had a reinforced gate that swung at the top on an old wagon axle. The bottom was whittled round and turned on a smooth stone. There was no doubt in his mind, even before he saw the two rotten, torn old cavalry saddle-blankets thrown indifferently across the corral bars, that white men lived there.

Jacob Harter's remark about renegades being with the Indians came back with new meaning. Jess had been wrong. This cabin definitely was inhabited by white men. That meant there *were* renegades with the hostiles. That also would account for the clever treachery that had been behind the attack on Clybourne.

He had to make a huge circle to get clear of the cabin, and just before he swung west seeking the tracks he was following, again, he paused briefly on a hillock and looked for his pursuers. There was no sign of them. Possibly they had concluded he was one of the white men who lived in that cabin. At any rate there was no sign of them.

By the time he found the shod-horse tracks the light was fast fading. With a worried look he tried to surmise their distant goal. In a general direction they were going toward Camp Lincoln, all right, but there were probably dozens of other just as likely places they were making for, too, especially if it were an Indian that was astride the animal he was tracking.

Before it became too dark to see he had to make up his mind. Deciding against pushing on blindly in the hope the tracks belonged to Elizabeth's mount, he sought out a hill with a sprinkling of trees on it and rode up to the base of it. Slipping off the bridle and loosening the saddle, he hobbled the chestnut horse, took his carbine and toiled up the ridge and sat down, waiting for the darkness to come and go.

An owl sailed by, low, his big eyes like bright pebbles under the water of a muddy stream. Jess watched him disappear rearward in the failing light, then swung his gaze out over the breadth and depth of the Sioux country before it got too dark to see. Nothing moved anywhere. He relaxed against a tree trunk and pushed his legs straight out in front of him, drew in a big breath and let it out, lay the carbine across his legs and sat there feeling strangely alone but peaceful.

The night was without end and he was at its mercy, but in a sense it was his friend and ally, for even if the Indians who had dogged his trail all the way from the forest were still after him, they wouldn't attack him in the dark even if they could find him.

Another day of it; then he'd know. Camp Lincoln was

athwart the old raiding trails into the upland valleys. He'd make it by early afternoon at the latest—barring unforeseen happenings—and if she was there . . .

With a start he remembered the letter her father had given him back at Ten-Mile. With one hand he felt for it, found it and drew out its crumpled remains. Running a finger under the flap, he ripped it open. The tearing paper made a sound that seemed as loud as a troop of cavalry riding down a dry-wash. When he unfolded the paper it, too, made a racket. He had to bend far over to see the writing. There wasn't much to it—but enough.

"Dear Jess:

A man with courage and wisdom adjusts to everything. A man with just courage fights—usually against adjustment—first; himself second; and anything else third—in this case I mean the Indians.

Elizabeth"

She had underscored the first "and" with two bold strokes of her pen. He read it over twice, folded it very carefully and put it back into his pocket, gazed up at the blanketing darkness and thought about it.

CHAPTER VI

BEFORE DAWN HE WAS ASTRIDE AND RIDING AGAIN. The watery gloom helped considerably. The obscurity guarded his passage and made the dry grass dew-damp, muffling the sound of his horse's hoof-fall. Feeling more secure than he had since leaving Clybourne, it freed his mind from some of its worry about his own danger and considered Elizabeth's plight. He knew he would cut the sign of the shod horse again as soon as it was bright enough to see the ground.

The farther he went the more his spirit accepted the possibility that she might have gotten through. Then daylight came reluctantly and he began to quarter, riding back and forth in a zigzag pattern, seeking tracks. When he found them it was necessary to dismount, lead his horse and walk head down to make them out. There was only the broken stalks of curing grass to show the faintest of horseshoe outlines. It was slow and painstaking work, but by the time the sun was up he could make them out well enough to notice with a deepening sense of fear and doubt that the rider he was tracking was no longer alone.

There were two other riders, one on each side, paralleling the first rider. His heart sank when all three of them swung abruptly eastward, away from Camp Lincoln, not more than half a day's ride ahead now.

He mounted his horse and took a long look behind and all around. There was nothing as far as he could see in any direction. No pursuers, no whiff of breakfast-fire smoke, no camps. The land lay silent, sun-washed and dead. His worried gaze went down to the three tracks again.

The implication was simple enough. If the tracks he'd been following were the girl's, she'd been captured. If they weren't, he'd been following an Indian on a trooper-horse. Sitting there thinking, he concluded that after coming this far it would be useless to turn back and try to pick up a new set of shod tracks.

He had to hope, then, that the solitary tracks were hers and that she had been captured. Accordingly, he swung eastward and booted the chestnut horse into a long, smooth lope, following the three sets of tracks.

91

What deepened his puzzlement was that, at a buffalo wallow where the earth had been churned to powder-fine dust, he saw three perfect sets of imprints. Every one of the horses was shod. The perplexity in his heart grew stronger.

Riding fast, he made for a high, brush-cluttered knob of a hill. Riding up it, he angled and dismounted close to the summit. He went the last hundred feet afoot and squatted on the skyline, hidden by the brush.

He saw them far off and grunted gutturally to himself. Evidently they'd stopped during the night, too, which was more than he'd dared hope for. Still, it made sense that they would need rest. The day before had been a long and hectic one for the Indians.

Studying the land ahead of the three riders, he plotted a course that would allow him to get around them unseen by staying to the breaks in the badlands. He remained there a moment longer musing, his glance pinpointed on the three dark specks creeping across the vastness. There was no way to tell from the distance whether they were three Indians, two Indians and a white girl, or three white men.

He picked his course carefully and fretted at the delay. Under the dazzling daylight his own peril increased tenfold every hour he lingered in the stirred-up hornet's nest Indian country. At any moment his own tracks might be picked up and followed, if they weren't already being followed. Also, Indian hunters might ride up on some knob of a hill for a look over the country and see him. A lone white man skulking in and out of the erosion gullies, obviously tracking three riders, would be the signal to every Indian within hearing distance of a gunshot to come running.

The heat became a torture before he completed his

92

huge encircling ride. The chestnut horse was dripping and Jess was in no better shape. But he made it and found some miserly shade in a deep break between two gentle slopes. There he left his horse, took his carbine and slanted up the south slope of the near hill, lying flat and peering over the rim.

They were at least a mile away. The sunlight was an ally though, for its sparkling clarity rendered visibility good. His eyes widened abruptly. The middle rider was a girl—Elizabeth thank the Lord—but what held him flabbergasted was that the other two were white soldiers. Their blue uniforms stood out darker for the perspiration that drenched them. Without a wasted moment he jumped up, trotted down to his horse, sprang up, slammed his carbine into the saddleboot and wheeled in a flurry of dust, riding down the lane between the two hills and out around the south end of his covert onto the prairie.

Instantly the three riders hauled up and sat motionless. One of the blue-clad men swung down and tracked Jess' progress with his carbine. The other one was slower dismounting. He and Elizabeth came to earth at the same time.

A shot rang out even as Jess waved his hat back and forth over his head without slackening his forward gallop at all. With a pained and startled curse he slid his horse to a stop and yelled. The rifleman fired again. He could see the other trooper's gun coming up and spun away in a flurry of spewed dust and chalky earth.

Out of range, he ran his right hand gingerly under his ribs. The slug hadn't more than stung him and torn his shirt, but it had come much too close. Enraged, he made frantic signals and called out his name. The troopers seemed to listen, then speak among themselves. Even

Elizabeth was consulted. When his indignation was at its peak, one of the soldiers turned back to face him and waved his hat beckoningly. With coldly angry eyes Jess urged his horse down toward them at a slow walk.

Riding indignantly toward Elizabeth and her companions, his fear was resurrected two-fold. In that atmosphere where sight and sound travelled miles, that solitary imprudent shot could have been heard by any number of roaming Sioux warriors.

He was still engrossed with this and the unexpectedness of the assault when he was close enough to see one of the soldiers bring his arm from behind him. He had a pistol in his grip. It was only partly seen and actually, if the sun hadn't reflected off it, he probably wouldn't have seen it at all.

His fingers tightened on the reins as he went closer; then, while he was still too far away to see their faces, both troopers raised pistols and fired. At the same instant Elizabeth's voice rose in a wild scream.

Without a sound or a flinch, Jess' chestnut horse collapsed, catapulting his rider over its head. He rolled instinctively, clawing for his pistol, spitting sand. A rider was racing toward him. He flung himself belly down, threw up his own gun and snapped a wild shot that missed. The trooper veered off and slammed two shots back.

Jess rolled back behind his dead horse, flung off the sweat that was mingled with fine, abrasive dust, and hugged the ground. Elizabeth cried out indistinctly again. He started to raise his head. His vision was obstructed by the canting butt of his carbine. With a wild tug he unbooted the weapon, laid it across his askew saddle and fired. The racing trooper's horse went down in an earth-spraying sprawl. The man rolled like a log and tried to get up. Twisting painfully, he inched close to the dead animal and hid behind it.

The second trooper, with Elizabeth beside him, holding the reins of the two horses, knelt with his rifle snugged in against his shoulder.

Jess saw the pale flash of a muzzle blast and heard the deep roar of the rifle. His own carbine, short-barreled as it was, didn't have the range of that rifle. He held his fire and lay flat.

Unreasoning anger obscured the astonishment he had felt when they downed his horse. Now, far back in his mind, was a shred of suspicion. It was perfectly understandable that soldiers alone in Indian country should be nervous and quick-triggered, but that they would carry their uneasiness to this extreme was doubtful.

The trooper behind the dead horse squeezed off a shot. Jess couldn't see him. The bullet went a little wide and threw up a spout of dun dust. Jess scorned firing back until the man had fired three more times; then, more in irritation than anything, he dumped a long shot into the dead horse's carcass. For a while after that the second trooper was quiet.

"Get up, Swindin! Stand up and throw those guns down!"

Jess peered over his horse's back at the kneeling rifleman over by Elizabeth. The man's weapon sagged. His flushed face was visible above it but the features weren't clear at the distance.

"Come on out! All this shooting'll bring the Sioux. Throw down your guns and walk over here."

Jess risked raising his head. The man behind the dead horse still wasn't visible. Elizabeth was sitting her horse beside the other soldier.

"You darned fools," Jess called back. "What's the

matter with you? Don't you recognize a white man when you see one?"

"How you goin' to tell," the rifleman called back, "when half the Indians're wearing white-man clothes? Come on out."

Jess holstered his hand-gun and clutched his carbine lightly. He looked over to where the hidden trooper was. "Call your friend out first. I want him in plain sight—no bushwhacking."

The rifleman stood up and leaned on his gun. "Mike, come on out."

For a long time the second soldier didn't move. Then very slowly, gingerly, he raised up a little at a time until he was convinced Jess wasn't going to fire, and finally started to hobble painfully away from his horse, heading toward the other soldier.

"Now, Swindin, come on."

Jess stood up gradually, still hanging onto his carbine. With a long, sad glance at the dead chestnut horse, he shuffled around its carcass and struck out toward the two soldiers and Elizabeth. With instinctive alertness he raked the landscape with a probing and unfriendly glance. If there were hostiles within several miles, they would surely be streaking it toward the sounds of the fight.

Elizabeth was motionless. He could see the high burnish of her color and the deep circlets of blue under her eyes. A slower, more malevolent, bleak gaze went to the two soldiers. One was about his own height and weight, while the other was shorter but stockier. When he was almost up to them the big soldier, still leaning on his rifle staring at Jess, straightened up and blew out a long sigh.

"That was bungled, Swindin." Both of them stood there staring at him. The shorter man was favoring one

96

ankle by standing hip-shot. His stare was violently antagonistic. Jess returned glare for glare.

"Bungled? Why, you fools, you might've killed me. As it is you've set me afoot."

The big man nodded stoically. "Sure have, haven't we?"

Jess stopped, wide-legged, in front of them. "Don't sound so complacent about it, soldier. One of you'll walk back, not me. I give you my word on that."

The big trooper's thin mouth cracked a little in a humorless smile. "Is that so?" he said. "Back where—to Clybourne?"

"You're not from Clybourne. You're from Camp Lincoln, aren't you?"

Then, for the first time, his suspicions grew into conviction. They weren't soldiers at all. He had been fooled by the uniforms. His eyes flickered over the blue cloth, the campaign hats and belts, the sidearms and the rifles. Soldier equipment all right. None of it would have been hard to acquire after the defeat and plundering of Fort Ten-Mile.

"Lincoln?" the big soldier said; then he turned and gazed woodenly at his companion. "Are we from Lincoln, Mike?"

But the shorter trooper wasn't in the frame of mind for humor. His ankle had been sprained when his horse went down and pained him a good deal. "No, we're not from Lincoln. We're from Indian country, if that's what you're askin', mister."

Without speaking, Jess swung his head and stared at Elizabeth. She didn't reply to the question in his eyes; just nodded her head tightly.

Jess' eyes moved back to the big man's face. "You aren't soldiers?" he asked.

"That's right. How'd you guess it?"

"Who are you?"

Still cold-eyed and unblinking, the big soldier said, "Friends of the Sioux, Swindin. Just friends of the Sioux."

Jess was rooted. He hadn't believed it when Jacob Harter had told him of renegades being with the Indians. He still found it hard to believe even when the flesh-and-blood evidence stood in front of him in stolen soldier clothing.

"Renegades."

The short man flashed out with a scorching string of profanity, but his companion shook his head to silence him, never once looking away from Jess.

"Call it any name you want to, Swindin, I don't care. Just one thing interests me. How come you are ridin' from the north?"

Jess stared and didn't answer. Elizabeth spoke for the first time. "I told you he was coming back from taking the news to Camp Lincoln."

The short man propped his rifle, barrel down in the dust, butt-plate under his arm like a crutch, and squinted up at Jess. "That right, cowboy? How'd you get around the Indians?"

"I never saw any. A few far back were trailing me, but they gave up before sundown."

The big man began to wag his head firmly. "I don't believe you. This girl here was riding hard and she didn't make it. You mean to tell me you . . ."

"I'm saying just one thing, and you can believe it or not as you please. I'm on my way back to town after carrying the news of the massacre at Ten-Mile and the attack on Clybourne."

He made his stare as steady as he could and ignored

Elizabeth altogether, although she had given him his cue as to what to say.

The short renegade's mouth twisted. "In that case," he said slowly, "I reckon there's no sense in wasting any more time on him—is there, Starr?"

But the big man was thoughtful. It was quite clear that he had doubts both ways. His gaze was direct and pensive.

Jess turned toward Elizabeth. "Where did you pick them up?"

"About dawn," she said. "I was fooled by the uniforms just like you were."

Their gaze held through a long, silent moment; then Jess said: "I heard there were renegades running with the bronco Indians, but I didn't believe it."

The big man called Starr broke his long silence. "Didn't you?" he said evenly. "Well, now you know. What good's it going to do you?"

"I'm not worrying. I might have worried on the trip up, but not now."

"I think you're lying, Swindin. The girl recognized you right off, but she said you were with the column that went up to Ten-Mile."

"That's right," Jess said glibly. "I was. After what we found at Ten-Mile I rode for Camp Lincoln."

The big outlaw shook his head and a hard glimmer shone in his glance. "I know you're lyin' now, Swindin. A minute ago you said you had taken the news of what happened at Ten-Mile *and Clybourne* to Lincoln. If you'd left Ten-Mile for Lincoln, you wouldn't have known what happened at Clybourne."

Quickly, desperately, Jess said, "Wouldn't I have? The scouts out in the rear of the wagon train brought us word of the attack back in town. I went for help right then because we all knew Clybourne didn't have enough defenders."

He was perspiring copiously under his shirt and the heat didn't inspire all of it, either. Watching bleakly, he saw the nagging doubts return. The bluff wasn't working. The outlaw pursed his lips and stared. Silence settled ominously around them; then Mike spoke up.

"We're wastin' time, Starr. Kill him, or let's take him to Iron Shirt's camp and wring it out of him."

But Starr was shrewder than that. "Be too late then," he said. "If the blue-bellies are ridin' down from Lincoln, we've got to know before they come bustin' over some hog-back ridge."

"Let me work on him," Mike said quickly. "I'll get the truth out of him."

Starr regarded Jess almost gently. "Nope. That'd take too much time, too. Take his guns, Mike."

Jess' throat tightened and the breath ran out of his lungs in a low sigh. He watched the big renegade without looking at Mike at all. The shorter man hobbled forward with his one free hand holding a pistol. Disarmed, Jess waited with a sinking sensation. Even if he bluffed his way with these two it still didn't help the situation at Clybourne. While the search for Elizabeth had been uppermost in his mind he hadn't thought overly much for the town. Now, knowing she had come this close and no closer to help, and that the Indians didn't have her, the responsibiilty for getting aid weighed heavily on him.

"Mount up, Mike," Starr said. "Then take Swindin behind you. I'll ride up behind the girl."

Mike moved toward Starr's horse. The stirrups were too long, and he winced when his injured ankle struck the horse's side. "Where'll we take 'em—to the cabin or Iron Tail's camp?"

After Jess was behind Mike's saddle, Starr swung up behind Elizabeth. He reached around and took the girl's reins. "You ride a little ahead, Mike," he said, "and head northwest—toward Lincoln."

Mike's head came around swiftly. "What for? If those blue-bellies're out we might bump into 'em. Remember—we're riding double, Starr. We couldn't outrun a slow cow."

"Just stick to the ridges as much as you can," Starr said, unruffled, "and use your eyes—that's what you got 'em for. We want to make sure about the soldiers before we make a run for Iron Tail's camp. As riled up as the Injuns are right now, I wouldn't want to take them any wrong information about soldiers."

Understanding but still as reluctant as before, Mike reined northwestward without another word.

Jess threw Elizabeth a long glance and got back one, a resigned and despairing one, as though she were trying to tell him she understood and was prepared for the worst. He regarded the soldier coat in front of him for some time in glum silence, then craned his neck past Elizabeth to Starr. The big renegade was peering into the distance. Finally he swore at the coat he had to wear, caught Jess watching him and lapsed into thin-lipped silence.

They rode northwest until the sun was high overhead and blast-furnace hot; then Starr reined up beside Mike and Jess. "I've had about all I can take of this heat for a while. Let's make for the scrub-oaks yonder, Mike, and rest a spell."

They did, and the shade, though dappled and shallow, was a blessing. Elizabeth's face showed two dark red splotches under her eyes, and a waxen pallor.

Starr removed his blue tunic, and the filthy shirt

101

underneath was sodden. He looked at Mike with a limp expression. The shorter renegade's ankle was swollen now and bothering him more and more as time passed. He dropped to the cool ground under the trees with a grunt and a curse and looked at his pardner.

"Starr, whyn't we just find his tracks and follow them? They'd tell us enough, wouldn't they?"

Starr made a cigarette before he answered. Then, with smoke spilling listlessly from his nostrils, he said, "His tracks don't mean anything. What we want is to see soldiers or not to see 'em. If he's went up there they'll be riding now. If he didn't and says he did—there won't be a soldier beyond the camp's limits. That's all we want to make sure of."

Mike, made garrulous and disagreeable by the pain from his ankle and the muggy atmosphere, gazed unpleasantly where Jess stood. "I'd rather just leave him here for the buzzards to eat, then ride on over the hills toward Lincoln, see if he lied or not, then get back to the cabin. Jake and Martin'll be waitin' for us."

Again Starr dissented. "Nope. We'll deliver 'em both to Iron Shirt. Be the wisest thing we could do right now. It'll stop any talk the bucks might be makin' against us for what happened at Clybourne. Show 'em our hearts are strong sort of stuff. There's bound to be plenty mad bucks after Clybourne. Our position's not too darned strong at best, Mike. One defeat like Clybourne and we're skatin' on awful thin ice."

"It isn't that bad," Mike growled, worrying his boot off and probing his ankle gingerly. "Jake knows Sioux and Cheyennes like the inside of his hand. He says we're safe enough among 'em, at least until the soldiers get to botherin' 'em too much."

"Jake and Martin are thinking of the loot we're

picking up. It's blinding them."

Elizabeth was motionless and silent in the shade. Her eyes were fixed on the horizon southward. Jess was listening to the renegades talk with dawning interest. He went deeper into the shade and dropped down.

"Get a lot of loot out of Ten-Mile?"

Mike's malevolent glare was as hostile as his ankle was swollen. He said nothing.

Starr smoked thoughtfully before he answered. "Swindin," he said in a quiet, conversational voice, "you got an unusual name."

Jess looked at the outlaw appraisingly. Whoever Starr was and whatever he was, he certainly wasn't easily aroused nor inclined to fret and worry as his companion was.

"Real unusual name. Don't believe I ever heard it before—but once. Swindin, where you from?"

"Places," Jess said shortly. He was conscious of Elizabeth's eyes on him.

"Sure," Starr said drowsily. "Places. Like all of us— places. Only I got an idea you're from the States—way back up north in the States." The deep-set, bright, hard eyes moved to Jess' face and stayed there. "Chicago, maybe. How about it. You from Chicago, Swindin?"

With a suddenly cold feeling, Jess gazed steadily at the outlaw. "What made you pick Chicago?" he asked in a brittle way. "Is that where you heard the name before?"

"No," Starr said, "I've never been to Chicago. Never been east of the Missouri, Swindin. Nope; guess again."

Jess knew the man was baiting him. He also knew Starr had a reason, and he was afraid it might be a good one, for so far Starr had scored easily, and that was no coincidence. The States were large, the name Swindin

103

relatively uncommon. What could this renegade know? He knew positively he'd never seen the man before. It was possible Starr had seen him, heard of him somehow, but that was unlikely.

"I'm not good at riddles," Jess said. He made a cigarette and looked through the smoke at Elizabeth. She was still regarding him with a tired expression and unfathomable eyes. She had heard and was interested. That, too, annoyed Jess.

Starr let his gaze drift away, in a long sweeping study of the heat-cowed land, then back to Jess' face again. "No riddle; just one of those things, Swindin."

Annoyed, irritated beyond prudence, Jess said, "Like leading Indians against whites? Like working out a scheme to sack Ten-Mile and Clybourne?"

Mike's head came up. His gaze was like steel, but it was Starr who spoke, as usual, enigmatically, callously, and with a wispy smile.

"Yeah—like that, if you want. You figured it, huh? Well, good for you. It was good, wasn't it?"

The conversational, almost drowsy and indifferent way the man spoke infuriated Jess. "Good? Killing soldiers—women and kids—being the worst kind of a renegade there is? Yeah. That's good. You'll find out how good when the Army gets you."

"It won't," Starr said with maddening coolness. "Not much chance of that. We've got five thousand Indians in front of us. If they kill them—why then, I expect we'll just ride on—only they won't. Indians aren't easy to kill, especially when they got someone else to do their thinking for them and their planning." Starr looked steadily at Jess.

"But I didn't plan that, Swindin. Feller named Martin Goddard did. Ever hear of him?"

104

Jess' face seemed to close, to settle and darken. After a lengthy silence, he said in a low tone, "That's where you heard my name, isn't it?"

"Yes."

"Where is he? What's he doing here?"

"Doing here? Why, Martin's our brains out here. He's the lad who plans and thinks for the red-skins."

Jess was stunned.

"Where is he?"

"Well," Starr said in his unruffled way, "I reckon he's at the cabin by now. Should be; all he had to do was ride as far as Iron Shirt's camp, placate the old devil, then go on down to our cabin. That's where we was going when we stumbled onto the girl's tracks, followed them and picked her up."

Mike broke in petulantly. "Come on, Starr; he might've told the truth. There might be blue-bellies all over the country by now. Sittin' around here is bad."

"In time, Mike. It's mighty peaceful here in the shade." Starr looked over at Elizabeth. "Isn't it, ma'am?"

She didn't answer him. Jess turned his back on them all and walked out a little ways. He stopped just short of the wavering sun-scorch just as Mike drew his pistol and opened his mouth to say something.

Elizabeth looked at his back and saw the stooped slant of his shoulders. She got up and went over beside him. He ignored her until she spoke.

"Jess, what is it? What did he mean?"

He spoke without looking around at her. "A man named Martin Goddard's been telling him about me."

"But who is Goddard?"

"Who?" he said, turning, looking sternly down at her. "Goddard is the man who ran away with my wife while

105

I was in the Army. That's who he is."

Her face blanched in spite of the heat. He took a grim pleasure in saying it as bluntly as he could. She wanted to know. She thought he was a moral coward, running from himself. Well, he'd slam it at her as harshly as it had been thrown at him when he returned from the war and the Army.

"I was married before the war; then I was gone four years. When I came back my wife was gone; so was my home, my savings, my reason for believing in things and people. Martin Goddard was the man. I don't know him; never saw him. You've always wanted to know. Now you know."

"Jess . . ."

She didn't finish, and Jess wasn't listening anyway. He was staring off over the brassy plains a little southward, over about where he estimated the cabin would be. Without another glance at her he swung back toward Starr.

"Where's Goddard's wife?"

"Dead," Starr said easily, quickly, watching the recoil in Jess' face. "She died two years ago, down in the Strip. Malaria, Martin told us one time when he was drunk."

"Was that also the time he told you what her married name had been before?"

"Yeah. That's why I had a lot of curiosity to catch you alive. This girl here told us who you were. I figured Martin'd like to have you in front of him." Starr's smile was cruel.

Mike spoke without looking at Starr. "You'd like that, wouldn't you?" He sounded antagonistic.

Starr nodded candidly. "Yeah. I'd like to see Martin, the handsome ladykiller, stopped cold. This'll do it. It'll take him down a notch."

Mike got up with a curse and glowered at his companion. "I'm goin' on, Starr. You can sit here playin' cat and mouse if you want, but I don't like this. We're walkin' on eggs."

Starr shrugged and began to get to his feet. "All right," he said, "all right. You need a drink, Mike. Swindin, this time you walk. We've got to baby those horses a little."

Jess walked ahead of them, his clothing drenched with perspiration. His depth of bitterness kept him going. Starr would call directions, and Jess followed them in absolute silence.

It was thus that they came to the long, brushy ridge that Jess stopped atop of, staring out over the land northward, his eyes puckered and smarting from the sharp glare.

"Indians."

Starr slid off his horse with a grunt, trudged up beside his prisoner and looked. Mike didn't dismount. Jess could hear his horse fidgeting, as if the shorter renegade were set for flight.

It was a straggling line of heat-sapped Indians; men, women, and children, horses, dogs, travois, and flankers with medicine-shields, paint-streaked, sweating horses, and long lances that had limp feathers and scalp locks on their upper ends.

"Goin' west," Starr said musingly. "They aren't Iron Shirt's people. Not enough of 'em." He squinted. "You recognize 'em, Mike?"

"No!"

"Hummm," Starr said, relaxed in stance but intent in expression, completely ignoring the hostility in his companion's manner. "We'd best just let 'em pass."

They did, sweltering for an hour until the dust was

falling back where the Sioux had passed, then riding on again, with Jess still walking.

His mind was almost adjusted to the freakish coincidence that had put Martin Goddard near him. That Lorena was dead was a shock.

"Hold it, Swindin."

He raised his head and stopped. In the distance was a dark blotch that had to be a settlement of some kind. He heard Starr's grunt. The leather creaked. He turned and watched the lean outlaw get down heavily and look past him at the dark shadow in the distance.

"No life up there, Swindin. I guess you were lyin' after all."

Jess said nothing. So that was Camp Lincoln.

"All right," Starr said in a curiously detached way. "Let's head for the cabin. After Martin's through with you we can take both of you to Iron Shirt's diggings."

Mike turned his horse without waiting for Starr to re-mount. He was working his cracked lips savagely.

"Due south, Swindin," Starr said, springing up behind Elizabeth. "If you get too tuckered, you can ride and Mike'll walk a ways. Might do his ankle some good."

Mike's fierce explosion seemed to amuse the big renegade. He listened for a moment, then threw back his head and laughed. Mike lapsed into a silence as fierce as his outburst had been and rode along with lowered head.

CHAPTER VII

ELIZABETH AND JESS GOT A GREAT SHOCK WHEN THEY got to the cabin. In the late afternoon shade two renegades were sitting on a roughly made bench before the cabin, smoking, talking in low tones and watching their advance. Jess' eyes had blue specks before them when he stopped. His feet were puffy and lobster-red in his boots. He knew it without looking at them. Elizabeth was slumped and apathetic, with a hectic, feverish sheen to her face.

Mike swung down and hopped gingerly toward the sitting men, swearing with each step. Starr cared for the two horses, which were almost ridden down, before he sauntered over to where the others were, gazed at something lying in the shade, and dropped down on his heels.

Jess had seen the body of a man too. So had Elizabeth. That was what had shaken them. Both recognized him. Mike Leary—he of the bold eyes, dashing mustache, and testy disposition. He was dead. Flies were walking on him. The shade lay across one side of his exposed face. Elizabeth fainted when she tried to stand. Jess picked her up and staggered toward the bench. Four sets of hard, callous eyes watched him. His voice was a croak when he set her on the bench and looked up at Starr.

"Get her some water."

The renegade gazed downward thoughtfully, then shrugged and disappeared into the cabin. He brought back a gourd of tepid liquid and handed it to Jess. While Jess worked over Elizabeth, Starr squatted in front of his friends again, very deliberately made a cigarette, smoked it and gazed squint-eyed at a black-headed, dark-eyed, lean-faced man wearing dirty buckskin pants and shirt.

"Martin, we brought you back a surprise. An old friend of yours—at least an old friend of your wife's."

The dark-eyed man's calm gaze swung away from a dispassionate regard of Elizabeth. "No friend of . . ." He let it die softly, looking steadily at the squatting outlaw. For a space of several seconds he was silent; then his lips barely moved. "Starr—some day you're going to open your mouth and nothin's going to come out." Starr's steady, slitted look never wavered.

"Yeah? Maybe—maybe not."

"Cut it out, you two," the other renegade said irritably. "It's the heat. What you up to, Starr?"

Starr jerked his head toward Jess. "Him," he said. "That's Martin's dead wife's husband."

The sinewy body stiffened perceptibly, then Goddard's head swung slowly for a long look at Jess Swindin. His stare was impassive, cold as ice, a little pained, even, but he said nothing.

Jess had heard, and ignored them. Elizabeth was lying against him, conscious but with her eyes closed and the feverish color as high as ever. He raised his glance and met Goddard's stony look. Neither of them spoke.

Starr broke the impasse by flicking a hand toward the dead man. "Who's that, Jake?"

Mike was frowning at his bluish ankle. The man beside him shifted his seat a little, turned and regarded the corpse. "That? Darned if we know. He was captured at Clybourne by Iron Shirt's bucks. When they got this far they dropped him off. Must've racked him a little. He was almost dead when we got back."

Jess said, "His name's Leary."

Goddard was still looking at Jess and saying nothing. Starr looked around at him. "You know him?"

"No. Only to nod to."

Then Goddard spoke, ignoring the conversation about the dead man. "Where were you when Mike and Starr got you, Swindin?"

110

"Coming back from Camp Lincoln," Jess said doggedly.

Casually, almost blandly, Starr said, "He's a liar. We rode up by Lincoln, and there's not a soldier ridin' out anywhere."

Goddard remained silent, studying Jess. Elizabeth sat up and looked straight ahead. Jess put an arm around her, felt the limpness of her body and pulled her over closer so she could lean against him.

"You want me to take him over to Iron Shirt, Martin?" Starr asked.

Mike looked up briefly from his swollen ankle. "Take him to hell," he said. "He shot my horse from under me and I got a sprained ankle out of the fall. I got a claim on him for that."

Goddard finally looked away from Jess. His face was shiny and copper-colored. "Maybe tomorrow, Starr. Not right now."

Starr hid a cruel smile by lowering his head a little. The brim of his hat hid his eyes. He was brutal and vindictive and cruel in a cold, detached way. This pleased him very much, seeing Martin Goddard racked by old memories.

The renegade called Jake watched Mike make a boot-bandage out of a big bandana handkerchief. "Heck of a note," he said impersonally.

Mike looked at him with a nod. "Wouldn't have happened if Starr hadn't played it cute. We was goin' to let Swindin get in close, then drop him."

"You fired first," Starr said calmly.

"Well, why didn't you let me have him afterward?"

"I figured Martin might want to talk to him, that's why."

Goddard's dark eyes were fixed on Starr's features in

a blank, bleak way. "Thanks," he said dourly. "Now forget those two for a while. Iron Shirt's all stirred up."

"About Clybourne?" Starr asked.

Goddard wagged his head. "No, not especially. He's too much of an old battler to let that throw him. He's still too pleased over Ten-Mile. He's sent out word to all the other tribesmen about his victory over the fort and wants to carry his war right on down the line and run all the whites out of the country."

"He can't do it," Mike said bluntly. "Let the Indians whip one puny little fort and they think they can whip the United States."

"We don't care what they think," Martin Goddard said. "I think we ought to let 'em try it."

Starr was silent, smoking and watching Goddard. Mike was looking at him without blinking, waiting. He had a grudging respect for Goddard's plans after Ten-Mile and Clybourne. The scrawny, older man named Jake just sat there, staring straight ahead, saying nothing.

"Let them go," Goddard went on. "We'll ride along and pick up everything worthwhile we can, like we've been doing. Then, when they've about shot their bolt, we'll high-tail it west. It'll work just about like we thought it would."

"That's sense," Starr said. He looked at Jake. "What do you think?"

"I'm for it. We talked it over before you an' Mike come back."

"Mike?" Goddard said without looking around.

"Yeah, I reckon; but what about these?"

Goddard's head turned farther. He saw Elizabeth, and beyond her stood Jess. He said: "Iron Shirt can have them." In a thoughtful way he held his gaze on them both, then let it focus entirely on Jess. After an

112

exchange of silent looks, Goddard arose. "Come on, Swindin."

Jess didn't want to leave the girl but he did, following the renegade leader around the cabin where a pole corral trailed off irregularly toward some trees and a corner of the gravel-bar by the creek.

Martin Goddard stopped in the shade, turned and watched Jess come up. He appraised him, then leaned against a tree, his dark eyes pensive. Without preamble he said, "You'd like to kill me, wouldn't you?"

Jess considered it. "I don't know. I suppose so."

"I loved her."

Jess looked into the dark eyes and shook his head. "Not for that," he said. "Lorena was a woman. You couldn't have made her do anything she wasn't willing to do."

Goddard seemed a little surprised; then he got a cynical expression on his handsome face. "High and mighty, aren't you?"

"Just human, which you aren't, Goddard. Tell me something—how did you do it, at Ten-Mile?"

"That was easy. We made Iron Shirt strike his camp right in front of the soldiers and straggle away like he was giving up in disgust. Then Jake, Starr, and I rode down there—white men. They let us in and were glad for the extra guns. We cut the gate guard's gullet and opened the gate. The Indians were up close in the dark. That was all it took."

Jess watched the smooth face and the brooding dark eyes. This was no common killer. Goddard's expression was hawkish but not murderous-looking. His eyes were calm, his mouth full but not bitter. He could have been anything but what he was. In the Sioux dress he could have been a scout, an interpreter, a trapper—anything.

113

There were no outward signs of the man's warp at all.

"Why? Did you know there were kids in there? Kids and women?"

"Sure. What of it?"

Goddard seemed to derive an inner, ironic satisfaction from Jess' look. He tossed his head a little. One hand rested lightly on his holstered pistol.

"I'm up here for gold—all I can carry. So are the others. This way we get it. You can't get hung for killing a hundred people any quicker'n you can for killing one. It's bigger stakes, is all."

Jess said nothing. He felt no great loathing for Martin Goddard. Instead, he was awed at the man's unbelievable coldness. How could Lorena ever have stayed with a man like this?

"She died of malaria, Swindin, down in the Strip."

"Starr told me that."

Goddard's eyes, for the first time, narrowed just the slightest bit. "Starr's going to play it too clever one of these days. Well, I reckon you never missed her much, anyway."

Jess regarded Goddard impassively.

"You don't marry a woman without caring a lot about her, Goddard. I missed her. We'll leave it at that."

"All right. I miss her too."

Jess thought: "*In your way, I suppose you do.*" What he said was, "What are you going to do with us? Me and this girl from Clybourne?"

"Give you to the Sioux."

"Why don't you shoot us right here?"

"Because the Indians insist on all prisoners."

Jess knew it was hopeless. Somehow, miraculously, nature had left every decent impulse out of this man's constitution. He was so devoid of ethics, of standards

114

and scruples, that he was totally oblivious to them.

"Why'd you tell Starr and Mike you'd roused up the soldiers at Lincoln?"

"That's a fool question," Jess said, and paused before he answered. "Because I hoped it'd scare the lot of you into staying away from Clybourne and make you swing over to the defensive."

"The soldiers don't scare us. Jake and I rode up there and stole four horses the night before we snuffed out Ten-Mile. There," Goddard said, "see that big bay gelding with the numbers branded on his neck?"

Jess turned. The horse indicated was drowsing among the other four animals, over close to the cabin. "Yeah."

"That's one of them. Stole him right out from under the horse-guard's nose to show the Sioux we could do it. We kept him and the black there. We gave the Indians the others."

"How about the animals from Ten-Mile?"

Goddard's gaze came back to Jess' face. "The Indians got 'em. What'd we want with a big herd of horses? The Indians took everything but the gold, rings, stuff like that. That's our share for throwing in with them."

Jess sagged a little, looking at the calm, unwavering eyes of Martin Goddard. "Let's go back," he said, feeling empty, helpless and drained and frustrated. He and Martin Goddard were so far apart in all things it was senseless for him to prolong the conversation.

Goddard shoved off the tree. "Take you over to Iron Shirt's camp now, but it'll be dark pretty quick. We'll go over first thing in the morning." They walked back toward the front of the cabin side by side. In a conversational way, Goddard said, "Who is that girl?"

"She lives in Clybourne with her father." It was the only thing he could think of. "Give her a chance,

115

Goddard." He realized it was the poorest argument he could use with the renegade, knowing a ransom was in the back of his mind.

Goddard's reply was what he expected. "I might gamble on it, but I don't think the others will. Chance? Why? Because she's a woman?"

Starr was watching them guardedly when they took their places on the bench. He didn't speak, and none of the others did until the skinny oldster named Jake got up gingerly, stretched and spat.

"I'll rassle up some chuck. Starr, help me. Mike's out of cookin' for a spell."

Starr and Jake went inside. Mike was sitting dourly, smoking. After a bit Martin Goddard got up too. He went inside without raising his glance off the ground. Elizabeth was probing Jess' face with her eyes. In a voice too low for Mike to understand, she said, "What happened, Jess?"

He was sunk in a deep apathy. Goddard had affected him that way. Strangely, contrary to what he'd thought he'd feel, there was no unreasoning hatred for the outlaw. It was hard for him to define his feelings exactly. There was loathing, yes, and a hard core of repugnance, but Goddard was an impersonal enemy, like a rattlesnake. He was full of despair. That, more than anything else, sapped him, draining off the fury and blunting it.

"Jess?"

"He's going to keep us here tonight because they're too worn out to ride. Tomorrow we go to the Indians."

She lowered her eyes. "It would be better if they'd shoot us right here."

"I told him that. He said they had an agreement with the hostiles to turn over all prisoners."

116

"Quit mumbling," Mike said suddenly, glowering.

Jess threw him a withering glance and didn't even bother to reply.

"Is he who you thought he would be?"

"Yes. He's the man. That what you mean?"

"Yes. Jess, did my father give you a letter?"

"At Ten-Mile. I stuffed it into a pocket and forgot all about it until last night. Then I read it. You were right enough, Elizabeth only it doesn't apply to me. I'm not running from anything—her memory or anything else. It's just that I've no reason for staying anywhere. Nothing to tie me down—no folks, no kinsmen that I know of—no wife."

The shadows took the curse of heat away considerably. She made an effort to pat her hair into place and smooth her dress.

"Was she very young, Jess?"

"Why don't you forget her?"

"I can't."

"She was twenty when I went to war."

"And he is handsome, Jess. Don't blame her too much. She was alone. Four years is a long time—and he is good-looking."

"Is he?" Jess said in a flat tone of voice. "So are hundreds of men. Are women built so they can't stand being alone? How about me—how about the thousands of other soldiers? We were alone—worse than that. Our world was falling down around our ears. Did we run to the first woman we saw—the first pretty face?"

"You were strong. There's a difference."

"I don't want to talk about it any more, Elizabeth."

"All right," she said quietly. "Anyway, it's all long past, and I don't think it'll matter to either of us much longer."

117

He turned and gazed down at her. "Why should it matter to you anyway?"

"Because," she said gravely, "I'm in love with you, that's why, and it's like having your heart torn out—knowing all this."

He beheld her without moving or speaking. He was startled but not stunned by what she had said. Even so he couldn't think of an answer.

They were sitting like that when Mike got up and tentatively tried out his boot-bandage. Apparently the thing worked, because he hobbled past them twice without swearing or looking any meaner than was his normal wont.

Jess eyed the renegade's progress stolidly. The wheels were turning in his mind. Anything was better than sitting there docilely.

Elizabeth too, watched the renegade's progress. When he was at the cabin door peering in at his companions, she said, "Jess, I have a gun."

He gave an involuntary start.

"They gave me a big Dragoon revolver before I left Clybourne, and I took my own derringer. When I was captured they took my big pistol, but I still have the derringer. Do you want it? It's double-barreled."

"Lord no," he said fervently. "Not right now. Where is it?"

She touched the front of her dress. "Here."

"If we get a moment alone," he said in a tight voice, "give it to me then. In the meantime act as though you're bushed from the heat. And listen, Elizabeth, I've an idea. It's probably no good, but it's the best I can curry up right now. Here, take this stub of a pencil. I don't have any paper. After we eat, ask Goddard if you can go around in back of the cabin for a minute. I'm

118

gambling that he'll let you, thinking you'll want to have a moment's privacy. If he does, and if you go alone, tear a piece out of your blouse—anything you can write on—write 'cabin' and the word 'help' in big letters, sign your name and braid the cloth into the mane of the big bay horse that's around there in the corral, then open the gate and let him out.

"You'll have to work fast and it may not work, but it's better than sitting here waiting to be handed over to the Indians."

"But what good will it do to turn the horse loose?"

"They stole him from Camp Lincoln just before the attack on Ten-Mile, Elizabeth. When he's loose he'll head for home. If he makes it, the soldiers up there will find the note in his mane."

She turned furtively and watched Mike over by the cabin doorway. He was talking to the three renegades inside.

"Don't do that," Jess said. "Act natural."

"I'm sorry. I think I can do it, if they'll leave me alone for a few minutes. Do you think the soldiers from Camp Lincoln will come?"

He scowled. "The whole thing is a gamble, Elizabeth. I hope they come, that's all."

She looked up at him. "I feel much better all of a sudden."

"I don't," he said candidly.

Mike turned from the doorway and regarded Jess and Elizabeth with unfriendly eyes. "Come on, you two—time to eat."

The cabin was lighted by crudely made candles rolled by hand that smoked fitfully with a strong, musky odor. Jake and Starr cast their prisoners the briefest of glances. Martin Goddard eyed Jess steadily for a

119

moment, then slid his glance to Elizabeth, but it didn't linger long. Mike crowded down beside Jess at the rough table made of split logs, and used his belt knife to spear antelope steaks.

When they were all eating, Jess looked across the table at Goddard and said, "How do you know the Indians won't turn on you?"

Goddard grunted around a mouthful of meat. "We take that chance for the pay we get. It's a risk, but we don't expect to take it much longer."

Starr said, "You talk too much, Martin."

"Why? What's the difference? When Iron Shirt gets him, it won't matter what he knows."

Jake fixed Jess with a wondering eye and said: *"How kola, mita koda."* Jess shrugged. Jake then motioned toward the antelope steaks and said with a sardonic grin, *"Sunka tanka zi, yuta lela waste."*

"Save it," Jess said shortly, and went on eating.

Jake winked at Martin Goddard. He, of the renegades, had lived with the Sioux and knew their language. Goddard threw a witheringly triumphant glance at Starr.

"Satisfied?"

Starr didn't answer. He went on eating.

Jess kept his head down. Starr had made one mistake; a common one with the victorious. He underestimated his enemy. Jess couldn't speak Athabascan—but he knew *wibluta*—sign talk—the lingua franca of the Plains. Not, he reasoned, that it would do him any good once he and Elizabeth were delivered into the hands of the Sioux and Cheyennes. He ate desultorily, casting in his mind for a likely way of succeeding in an attempt to escape. None would come to him.

Goddard was swiping his mouth with a sleeve when Elizabeth made her request in a small, humiliated voice.

120

Jess looked at her once, saw the brick-red color and the unswerving look toward Goddard, and lowered his eyes. He chewed on a mouthful of meat that almost gagged him, and his breathing was shallow for the space of several seconds.

Goddard was still looking at her when the wizened old-timer, Jake, made a careless gesture with his sheath-knife. "Go ahead, lady," he said. "You wouldn't get a half-mile before some mounted warrior got you, if you was thinkin' of runnin' off. You know what bucks do to white women when they catch 'em?"

Goddard's dark eyes flicked to Jake and back to Elizabeth. He made a careless movement with his shoulders. "Sure," he said, "go on."

Elizabeth walked out with a wooden gait. Jess deliberately refrained from looking after her. Starr belched and wiped his knife on his pants leg, sheathed it and groped for his tobacco sack. When the smoke was curling up he looked speculatively at Goddard.

"You and Iron Shirt lay any plans for the next few days?"

"Sure we did. Why?"

"Just wondered. What are they?"

"We are going to make a fire-raid against Clybourne from both ends and both sides of town."

"They won't fight in the dark," Jake said, "so we got 'em set to burn the place."

Mike finished eating. He was feeling much better and looked almost pleasant when he gazed at Jess. "She's kind of pretty, Swindin."

Before Jess could answer, Jake raised his head slowly. "Don't get no ideas, Mike. Recollect what we agreed. No whites who see any of us are to live. That fits her like anybody else."

121

Mike got a sullen expression and said no more. Starr was still watching Goddard. Jess thought he looked like a cougar ready to spring. Definitely, Starr was jealous of Goddard's influence with the others.

"What do we do, Martin—follow 'em and help out?"

"If the fire gets a good set the whites'll have to abandon the place. That's what Iron Shirt thinks. He can catch 'em evacuating and make up for yesterday's defeat." With a shrug Goddard added; "It might work."

"There's a good chance of it," Jake said. "Anyway, I think, after this strike, we ought to split up and ride on. News'll travel fast about Ten-Mile. The government'll have blue-bellies swarmin' over the country as fast as they can send 'em down here."

"The Indians," Mike began to say, "are plenty strong. They'd give the . . ."

"That's foolish," Jake said scornfully. "Don't sop up all that strong-heart stuff the Indians hand you, Mike. If they ever get the Army down on 'em in force, they'll fade away like shadows. Don't kid yourself about that."

Goddard turned his liquid brown eyes on Jess. "How many soldiers were there in that train out of Clybourne?"

Lying glibly, Jess said, "About eighty, I reckon. I don't know for sure."

Jake snorted. "Eighty, nothin', Martin. Remember—I was the feller who slipped into town when they was gettin' the train ready and listened to the talk. There wasn't no more'n twenty, if that many."

Goddard was gazing at Jess when Starr spoke in his calm, casual way. "I told you he's a liar, Martin. You ought to know better than to ask him anything. He'll just stretch it for all he's worth."

Elizabeth came back into the room. Jess' heart skipped a beat. There was a flat silence while the girl sank down on the bench beside Jess again, scarlet-faced. Before anyone made a remark Jess spoke.

"Twenty or eighty, Goddard, you'll never sack Clybourne." There was conviction in his voice that even startled him. Four sets of eyes gravitated toward him.

"Why not?" Goddard asked silkily.

"Because you couldn't do it before when almost all the fighting men were with the wagon train and there were only boys and old men to stand you off. How are you going to do it when the town's alerted and chock-full of men with their backs up?"

Goddard's reply was thoughtful. "We lost only one thing at Clybourne, Swindin: surprise. Maybe we can't count on that too heavily this second time, but we can set the place afire all right."

Goddard leaned on the table with both elbows. "And something you don't know is that Iron Shirt's victory at Fort Ten-Mile was what the Sioux needed to get all their shirt-tail relations to come a-running. There'll be more buck-Sioux Indians hit Clybourne this time than you ever saw in one place before. They'll fire it and storm it both. Too bad you won't be around to see it."

Jake got up, sucking his teeth. He crossed the room where a set of built-in bunks lined one wall, turned and dropped down. Looking over at Mike, he said, "Your ankle hurts too bad—I'll feed for you."

Jess' breath caught in his throat. Something he had overlooked: the feeding of the corraled horses.

Mike twisted on his bench and started to rise. Starr stood up and yawned, stretched and spoke. "Don't worry; I pitched in enough feed for all of 'em when I put our stock up."

The sweat under Jess' shirt was running fast, and for a moment he thought he hadn't heard Starr right. Goddard jolted him out of his thoughts as Elizabeth came back in.

"You and the girl lie on the floor. We'll tie your hands and feet. Every one of us is a light sleeper, Swindin. Either of you make a move and you'll get your skulls cracked." He didn't say it as if he meant it especially, but Jess knew that in spite of his casual tone he wasn't being casual at all. He'd kill either one or both of them just as calmly, as unemotionally, as he'd said he would.

That was the key to the man's success thus far. No tension robbed him of his craftiness. No fear or conscience, no scruple or agitation, would rattle him. He was the deadliest kind of a man.

Starr tied them both as impersonally as though they'd been sacks of grain. He did it right, like a man would who'd done lots of rope work.

Jess lay still and relaxed. His feet ached. They were swollen in his boots and his clothes were stiff from salt-sweat, but his heart pounded in a sluggingly rhythmic way and his thoughts were on the Camp Lincoln horse.

He tossed a little and rolled onto his side. Elizabeth was watching him. When their glances crossed she smiled wryly, then dropped one eyelid very slowly and raised it. He didn't try to return the smile, just raised his eyebrows and asked in a whisper, "Did you?"

"Yes."

She wanted to say more—he could see it in her face—but she didn't. A monotonous, sing-song kind of cursing filled the silence. Jess knew without bothering to roll over and look that it was the man with the injured ankle. A garrulous voice he identified as belonging to

124

the older man, Jake, said, "Why don't you soak the thing in cold water, Mike? The swelling'll go down."

Mike's cursing sputtered into dour silence; then he sighed. "Too dark out now. Maybe in the mornin' if it isn't no better."

Martin Goddard coughed softly and kicked off his boots. Jess heard them fall. Someone was blowing out the candles; then Starr's voice came crisply into the stygian gloom.

"Martin, let's ask Iron Shirt for a couple of bucks to keep watch around the cabin here."

Goddard laughed. It was a thin, taunting sound. "If he gave them to us, Starr, they might be the ones that'd slit our throats."

"Jess? Roll closer."

He made one complete roll and was close enough to touch her. Someone's voice in the dark growled at them; then Goddard's clear tones came evenly.

"Swindin? I wasn't fooling. Make another fault and I'll kill you and the girl both."

Jess' eyes glowed unpleasantly. "Don't lose any sleep waiting for us to make a run for it, Goddard. Even if we could, we're not that foolish."

Soothingly, Jake said, "That's usin' your head, cowboy. I didn't figure you for an idiot. Afoot, you wouldn't get a mile before you stumbled into Indians."

When Jake stopped speaking Starr's voice, furry and sluggish, sounded through the room. "Don't worry. They aren't goin' any place—not lashed up like I do it."

Elizabeth put her face very close to Jess. He could see every feature. Her eyes shone large and moist. "I did it, Jess. I used a piece of my skirt to write on. I tied the note in his mane in a big knot of hair. I was afraid to take time to braid it in."

"Did you watch him—which way he went?"

"It was too dark to see much, but the sound was northward."

Jess smiled at her. Scant inches separated their faces. "Have you ever been to Camp Lincoln?"

"Not since I was a little girl, a long time ago. Why?"

"If the horse gets there and if the soldiers find the note and come back, according to my figures they should show up about dawn, depending on how fast they ride."

She was silent, watching him. His whisper had been so low she'd had to strain to hear it.

"If they come here we're dead ducks unless we can get loose, though."

She whispered, "We've got all night."

He said nothing. They had all night, true, but he'd tried Starr's intricate lashings. There was no slack anywhere. He recalled Starr's remark about them not going anywhere the way he tied people, and was inclined to agree with the renegade.

"Go to sleep, you two." It was Goddard. His voice was as firm and alert as ever. Jess swore under his breath. Didn't the renegade ever sleep?

He rolled his head on the earth floor and didn't see the quick look of anxiety in Elizabeth's glance as he looked away from her.

There had to be a way out.

The moonglow moved infinitesimally until a jagged pattern of it lay across his lower body near the doorway, making unrelated patterns. One was a bent horseshoe, another looked like a man's fist. Closer, near his shoulder, was the perfect outline of a moccasin. He gazed at it with detached interest for a while; then his look sharpened, becoming more bright and awake.

126

The idea was born of desperation and nothing else. Very methodically he traced the pattern with his nose. It took a long time to get it just the way he wanted it. Then, by diligent effort and much working of his teeth over his tongue, he dredged up saliva. Using his tongue on the dusty earth, he gave a slight dampness and a pressed-down appearance to the simulated moccasin track.

By then the moonwash had moved still farther down his body and was broken up and scattered into other small, meaningless shapes and patterns.

He rubbed his nose against his shoulder, spat to get the earthen taste out of his mouth, drew in a big breath and shouted: "Indians!"

The pandemonium that broke out was proof of how lightly the renegades slept. It was also proof how uneasily their heads rested in the blood-drenched land.

Guns appeared, winking in the soft light, and not a man said a word until they were standing above him. Martin Goddard stooped first. His face was sleep-puffy and his lips were pulled back from his teeth. Death was in his eyes.

CHAPTER VIII

"WHAT'S THE MATTER WITH YOU, SWINDIN? BAD dreams?"

The gloom hid part of Jess' face. He stared up into the hostile sets of eyes. "There was an Indian in here. When I yelled he ran."

"You're crazy," Goddard said, but he turned and bobbed his head at Mike. "Fetch a candle."

They saw the track without Jess showing them. Then

the silence grew more profound, more cloying and sticky. Goddard hunkered and studied it, then wizened old Jake. Starr and Mike looked at one another quickly, then out the open door. "Close it," Starr said.

Jake stood up, ran his tongue around inside his mouth and spat. Mike hobbled toward the door, and Jake wagged his head. "No sense t'that now, Mike."

Goddard was the last man to straighten up. He looked at Jake at the same moment Jess looked at Elizabeth. The girl's face was waxen, her eyes dilated and huge. She was silent, but the way the moon fell across her features was enough. She was terrified.

Mike burst out with a stinging epithet, looking at Martin Goddard. "I told you they might turn on us. Now listen, Martin . . ."

"You listen," Goddard interrupted sharply. "Get hold of yourself, will you? There's Indians about, we all know that. But if they'd been out to harm us they'd've done it before this."

"They would not," Mike exploded. "After Ten-Mile they couldn't do enough for us. After Clybourne you saw how they acted—sulky and mad-looking."

"All right," Goddard conceded. "There might be a few who're soreheads. But the ones that count, like Iron Shirt and the leaders, aren't against us by a darn sight."

Starr took Mike's side. Jess suspected he did it only because of his dislike and jealousy of Martin Goddard. "The chiefs wouldn't slit our throats—sure not—but it'd only take six or eight skulking sore-heads to slip in here while we were asleep and do it. Just one buck could do it, for that matter, and we all know there're bound to be some of those around."

"If not those," Jake added, "then some of the Dog Soldiers or the Bloody Custer bucks. No matter what the

128

chiefs tell them, there are plenty of bucks around who hate all whites, and that means us, too."

"I'm for getting out of here right now," Mike said fiercely. "Now—not in the morning."

Goddard's gaze had lingered on Starr before it flashed past Jake and settled on Mike. Jess watched them with a metallic sheen in his eyes. Goddard said, "Mike, you've been on edge for the last ten days. If we'd listened to you we'd've sloped long ago—about thirty thousand dollars ago—before Ten-Mile even. Well, we're not leaving just yet."

Goddard gazed at the moccasin track again, let his eyes wander from it to Jess, and linger there. He touched Jess' thigh with his boot and raised his head to the other renegades. "Iron Shirt'll find out who it was and tell them off after we deliver these two to him in the morning." The steady dark eyes fastened themselves on Mike for a moment. "And you—quit getting your wind up like an antelope every time you see something. Sure, there's danger all around us. We made it like that, to get loot. You knew what it'd be like, Mike. Get hold of yourself." Then the brown eyes swung to Starr and stayed there. No words came for a long time; then, softly, Goddard said, "Starr, you'd better buck up. I'm no kid. I know what you're doing."

Jess had never heard a more understated threat before.

Jake, as always, stepped in to smooth things over. "Let's don't get to frettin', boys," he said. "The second we're split up, we'll lose our strength. At best we're only four, don't forget. We got to work together and show a good face to the Injuns. When we're ready to pull out—all right—but now let's pull together. If we don't we'll more'n likely lose some hair, and I'm not joking with you. I know Injuns; they're like coyotes.

Most unpredictable people on earth—worse'n kids or wild horses."

Starr ignored both Jake and Goddard. He looked dourly at Jess. "What'd he look like, Swindin?"

"Britches and moccasins and naked chest and arms. Pretty good-sized buck."

"Any eagle feathers in his hair?"

"No, it was braided. I couldn't see too much of him, and when I thought he was going to bend over and knife me I let out the yell."

All of them stared at him thoughtfully; then Martin Goddard swore mildly and gazed out into the purple night where the moonwash was.

"Jake, you and Starr go look around. Mike, you take the first watch."

"And you?" Starr asked.

The brown eyes were impassively fixed on Starr's face. "I'm going to split up the stuff I brought back from Iron Shirt's camp and make four piles of it."

Starr looked sardonic. "In that case," he said, "I reckon we'd all best stick around until we get our shares—*then* take turns watching."

There might have been a fight then and there but for Jake. With an annoyed curse he swung between Starr and Goddard. "Come on, Martin. Divide up now. Let everybody see it's straight up."

There wasn't much else Goddard could do. Mike was left by the door while the loot was broken down into four equal shares and distributed. Jess, watching, saw Martin Goddard's swift upward glance at Starr as the rangy renegade pocketed his portion. None of the other outlaws noticed the look. They were too busy caching their loot.

Jake said, "Come on, Starr; let's go around the cabin

130

and down along the creek." He twisted his head toward Goddard. "You and Mike keep us covered, Martin. If there's assassins out there we'll need help."

"Sure," Goddard said, standing perfectly still watching the men cross the room. Jess could see the way his eyes were pinpointed on Starr's broad back. He was intrigued by what he had started with the fake moccasin print, until Elizabeth whispered to him.

"Jess, think of something fast. If the Indians don't get us along with these men, Jake and Starr will discover the horses are loose."

"Horses?" Jess said blankly, swiveling his head and gazing at her frightened face. "Did you turn them *all* loose?"

"I left the gate open. There wasn't time . . ."

"Oh, Lord," Jess breathed; then his mind put itself in the place of Starr and Jake. He pursed his lips and watched Martin Goddard stride past with a carbine in his hands, going over beside Mike at the door. The two renegades were too close—he dared not say what he was thinking even in a whisper—but he tried to look reassuringly at Elizabeth and wag his head warningly. There was nothing to say until Starr and Jake came back, but if his suspicion was right . . .

"Martin!" It was Jake, and for the first time there was a crimped tightness to his words. "The horses are gone!"

Jess saw Goddard stiffen. He swung a rapid glance at Elizabeth and smiled a little. His eyes were sharp and bright.

Mike said something that Jess didn't catch, then Goddard was speaking. His tone was up an octave, which meant he was troubled.

"Shut up, Mike, and cover me. Don't leave the cabin until we all get back."

131

"Wait . . ."

But Goddard, carbine held lightly, was hurrying around the corner of the cabin. Jess could hear Mike's breath whistling out of him. He flashed Elizabeth an eye-rolling look meant to indicate how close their call had been, then raised up a little.

"Mike, if you'll cut me loose and give me a gun I'll . . ."

"Wait until we see," Mike said in a surprisingly genial voice. "If they storm us, I'll cut you loose."

Jess had to be content with that. He lay back again, listening to the sounds outside. Minutes dragged by; then Starr and Jake came in abreast, with Martin Goddard lagging a step behind. Mike searched their faces.

"What'd you see?"

"Nothing," Jake said cryptically.

Starr, a little calmer, said, "It's too dark to read any sign out there, Mike, but they run off our horses all right. Left the bars down at the gate."

Mike made a choking sound and Martin Goddard stepped past him just then. Without more than a ripple of movement Goddard's long arm flashed out. The slap sounded loud and abrupt in the night. Mike gasped, and Starr turned with a twisted look.

"You had no call t'do that, Goddard!"

Mike was too startled to reach for his gun. Goddard was watching them both. His face was as blank, as cold and unconcerned as ever. "Now get your guts back," he said to Mike; then scornfully he went past the shorter, broader man and stopped six feet from Starr. Before any of them could speak, Jake was speaking from off to one side.

"Martin, Starr, I'll kill the first one of you that flicks an eyelash."

132

Without looking away from Goddard, Starr said, "You saw that, Jake. He had no call t'do that. Thinks he's a strong-heart warrior—the skunk. Well, I'm here to . . ."

"You're here for the same reason the rest of us are, Starr. Now straighten out of that and be quick about it."

Starr turned his head and gazed at Jake. So did Martin Goddard. The older man's lips were drawn back from his teeth. He held a long-barreled Dragoon pistol, cocked, in his right fist. There was no mistaking the look on his face, even in the sickly light.

Goddard relaxed and walked around Starr, dropped down on one of the benches at the table and gazed steadily at Jess.

Jake holstered his gun, shot each one of them a dark, angry look, and fished around for his tobacco sack. "You think it's Mike's nerves givin' out. You fools— it's all our nerves. You'd best see that and face it, or we'll be shootin' one another an' no one'll ride out of this."

Jess, watching the brigand's face, knew he was speaking more to Martin Goddard than to Starr, but Jess didn't think Goddard was upset. He thought he was disappointed about something. His expression looked it. Then Goddard dropped his bombshell.

"All right; forget it, Mike. I just wanted to slap you back into your wits. You spook too easy. Forget it." He lifted his glance and gazed at Starr. "You—simmer down. Listen; I don't think we'd better wait till dawn to get rid of these prisoners. If the bucks didn't shoot when we went out just now, it's because they're undecided. But they ran off our stock, and that means they're about ready to jump us. It's time we made a move of our own."

"Like what?" Jake asked.

"Go over to Iron Shirt's place and bed down with the old devil. Right in among 'em will be the safest place on earth after this. No matter how bronco a warrior is, he won't dast touch us in the old man's camp."

Jake pondered a moment, gazed at Mike and Starr and nodded. "That's pretty shrewd at that. What say, boys?"

Starr shrugged his indifference, and Mike was torn between his admiration for Goddard's planning, and fear of what might occur in the Sioux encampment if the warriors were all stirred up.

"Well," Goddard said testily, "say something."

"All right," Mike said, with difficulty.

"Be better walking too," Jake said. He nodded at the prisoners. "Let 'em up, Starr."

The six of them left the cabin when the moon was low in the sky. The night smelt heavily of cottonwoods, curing grass and parched, baked earth. It was a good scent. Jess plodded along beside Elizabeth, head down. His plan hadn't worked out too well, but after all, it had been only a diversionary tactic to break the monotony of waiting for what was certain to be ahead for them. What troubled him most was that they were walking away from the cabin. If the Camp Lincoln troopers were on their way, they'd find the place empty. It would be a long time before they'd have light enough to track the four renegades and their two prisoners.

He raised his head, swiveled it, looked long and searchingly for some vestige of dawn. He had no idea what time it was. Mike, hobbling gingerly beside him, also turned and looked.

"Be an hour yet before the sun's up. We'll be danged near to Iron Shirt's." He squinted past Jess at Elizabeth.

134

"Best time to walk or ride, right now. You won't get a sweat up." He seemed to consider something, then straightened up and said, "You won't ever get a sweat up again—you two."

Jake swung up on the far side of Elizabeth. He smiled at Mike's heavy jest and appraised the girl. "It won't be so quick for you. You look pretty strong to me."

Jess' blood pounded in his temples. He said nothing though, because he knew Elizabeth, puzzling over the innuendoes, was nowhere near guessing the truth.

Mike opened his mouth to pursue the topic, and Jess cut him off as he'd done once before.

"How far's this Sioux encampment?"

"Not far," Jake said conversationally. "Maybe five, six miles."

"Where're Goddard and Starr?"

"Martin's gone on ahead to scout a little. Starr's behind us, nosing around. If the bucks who stole our horses were watching they saw us strike out. If they rode ahead, which is more likely, Martin will scent them up."

"And if they attack?" Jess prompted, pleased in a grim way that he had fooled Jake who, alone among them, was obviously an old hand in Indian country.

"If they were going to make a run at us, Swindin, they'd've done it long ago. We've been targets for a couple of hours now. Nothing's happened."

Jess was suddenly alarmed by the cold, hard touch of something low along his side, where his hand lay. He felt for it with a leap of his heart. It was a tiny under-and-over derringer. It was heavy, too, despite its insignificant size. His finger wandered over its bore. He could almost get the tip of his little finger in each barrel. Probably .41 caliber. His breath came in tight gasps and

135

he forced himself to speak.

"How much would you and Mike take to let us go?"

"You don't have that much money, Swindin," Jake said easily, almost as though he relished the refusal. "Martin had an idea of ransom for the girl here. It's no good though. No matter what we got, you two could identify us. After Ten-Mile we can't have that for any amount of money. Forget it."

"You talk too much," Mike said sullenly.

"Do I?" Jess said scornfully. "Well, at least my knees aren't knocking together."

"Cut that out, Swindin!" Jake said in a thin voice, throwing a savage look after the words.

They walked on through the cool night, and Jess, looking ahead for a glimpse of Goddard, got a surprise. The sky was lightening. He turned fully and looked behind them. Trees and brush, even the distant mountains, were wanly visible. "It's dawn," he said aloud.

Jake grunted by way of reply, and Mike was totally silent. Elizabeth felt for his hand, squeezed it hard and let it go.

The weight of the derringer made his pants pocket sag. He feared it might be noticeable after full daylight.

"There's Martin," Mike said suddenly, with a rush of relief.

"Hold up a minute," Jake said, unconvinced and swinging his carbine to bear on the stalwart shadow approaching them. He bent a little and skylined the oncoming figure, straightened up after seeing the man's hat, and relaxed, setting the carbine-butt on the ground.

"See anything?"

Goddard's dark eyes flicked over them. He seemed to be out of breath and trying to control it. He stood wide-legged, shaking his head. "Not a thing. If they're around they must be behind us. Probably are. Starr come up yet?"

"No," Jake said. "He'll catch up pretty quick. Did you go far enough to see Iron Shirt's bivouac?"

"Too dark," Goddard said glibly. "Unless something's moving you don't see it. Anyway, I was looking for mounted bucks—not villages." His glance swept over Elizabeth and Jess again, thoughtfully; then he shrugged. "Let's go. Sun'll be up pretty quick. I'd like to be in the camp before it gets to cooking."

But something Jake was thinking bothered him. With a frown he said, "Let's wait for Starr. After daylight, alone like he is, he'd be a sitting duck for hostile warriors."

Goddard looked more annoyed than angry. "Starr can take care of himself. Come on. I'll have Iron Shirt send out after him if he isn't up with us before we make the camp, but he will be."

Persuaded but obviously still reluctant, and frowning in a puzzled way, Jake shrugged. "All right, but I don't like it." He threw his head up suddenly much as a startled animal might. "Listen!"

Jess stiffened. A shiver of anticipation ran through him. Mike, beside him, swung rearward with an outward whoosh of breath.

"Horses. Riders coming."

Mike's face drew into a curdled expression. Jess heard the riders only after Mike did. He swung to look at Jake and Martin Goddard. Neither of them saw him, for they were looking down the grey dawn, behind.

Jake let off a savage curse. "Martin, it's the whole tribe, from the sound. I'll give you odds they got Starr."

But Martin didn't answer. He and Jess were listening

137

to the same undercurrent of sound, faint, but unmistakable all the same. Evidently Mike was listening to the same thing. He suddenly drew himself up erect, ignoring his injured ankle, and said a word that had dread in it.

"Soldiers! It's the Army!"

"You're crazy," Jake snapped, but he bent a little, straining to hear better. Very slowly, gradually, he straightened up. "No, you're not, Mike. I can hear the metal."

Jess had heard the soft, whispering sound of metal scabbards when Mike had. His heart was in his mouth. It was still too dark to track, but the Army would find the cabin vacant and undoubtedly they'd have Indian scouts with them. They'd find the tracks and gallop over them. There was no hope for the renegades afoot unless they could get to the Sioux encampment fast.

Goddard's calm face was like dark leather with a beard-shadow. He rocked down on his toes again. A lot of the erectness seemed to go out of him. His heavy brows drew inward above his nose. "Swindin wasn't lying, Jake. There's your proof: the Army from Lincoln. They're back at the cabin sure as the devil."

But Jake was past caring whether Jess had lied or not. All he was concerned with was getting away. With an oath he spun toward Goddard and snarled, "Let's go!"

Mike prodded Jess, who felt for Elizabeth's hand and drew her along with him. They trotted under the frenzied urging of Mike's carbine. Jake and Goddard, less burdened than Jess was with Elizabeth, and faster than Mike with his taped ankle, fled ahead until they were only bobbing shadows in the distance.

Jess jogged with his jaws locked. His feet were swollen and hurting. He ignored them, watching the two

138

swiftly pacing shadows ahead. When the distance was great enough he dug for the little pistol, palmed it, drew it out and spun fast toward Mike, knocking aside the man's carbine and shoving the stubby barrel savagely into Mike's midriff.

"Now stand still. Don't make a sound."

Mike didn't. His eyes popped and his mouth sagged, but he stood like a statue.

Jess disarmed him and handed the Dragoon pistol to Elizabeth. He closed his fist around the carbine as if it were a club. With his other hand he turned Mike around, stepped back and swung the carbine by the barrel. The stock made a sickening sound when it came brutally against Mike's good ankle. The renegade let out a shrill scream and fell. Without a second's hesitation Jess struck him over the head. This time Elizabeth gasped.

"Jess!"

He turned, felt for her hand, ignored the horror in her face and began to run diagonally southward toward a great, shaggy shadow that was trees and undergrowth along a creekbed.

Beating their way deep within the clawing profusion of growth, Jess swung her behind him where a tiny clearing was, and beckoned for silence.

Behind them the dawn was as still as a deep pool.

He straightened up and turned toward her. "I tried to wreck his other ankle too. When he comes to he won't even be able to crawl far. They'll find him."

"It was so savage, though."

He curbed his answer in time, but the exasperation showed, and she flinched from it. "Can you be sure it's the Army, Jess? Couldn't it be Indians just as easily?"

"That's why I ran in here," he answered. "I'm pretty

sure it's the Army, but the Indians have soldier horses and equipment too."

"Martin Goddard and the one they call Jake didn't think it was Indians," she said.

"Maybe they didn't, but either way they don't want to be caught by a big war party, red or white."

"Will they come back for Mike?"

"I hope they do," he said slowly. "I hope they do, Elizabeth."

There was no time to say any more. The sound of a vast host of horsemen swelled with their coming. Jess put his hand on Elizabeth's arm and pressed downward. She dropped low in the rank grass. He didn't see the violent shiver that swept over her.

With just his head and eyes above the brush, he waited, hearing the advance but unable to see anything more than a long, swaying line of riders. The clanking sounds were more pronounced and, in spite of his knotted insides, Jess was confident it wasn't a war party of Sioux and Cheyennes. Then they swept still closer and he watched the Indian scouts trotting ahead of the column, bent almost double. There was a sense of urgency about the way the two Indians were studying the ground.

Without any warning both Indians dropped flat. Jess' scalp crawled. He could see the entire drama easily from where he squatted.

"*Wasicun!*" an Indian called out. "*Wasicun!*" (White man.)

The column changed its gait to a slamming trot and came up even with Mike's weaving, moaning silhouette.

"Jess! Oh, thank God—it's the Army!"

He stood up, hearing her rising behind him. It was the Army all right. He was weak in the legs from relief. "I

140

never was so glad to see uniforms in my life."

"Call to them. They've found Mike."

"Don't shoot, soldiers; I'm coming out."

One of the prone Sioux scouts leapt up with a trilling sound of warning and bolted. His back had been exposed to the place where the call had come from.

Jess waited until the ripple of tension had died down. "Do you understand me, up there?"

A deep, gravelly voice called back harshly, "We heard you. Come on out and hold your gun above your head."

He twisted to look at Elizabeth. She was crying soundlessly. Instinctively he bent a little and rubbed his beard stubble along one cheek, pulled back and smiled at her.

"Not now, Elizabeth, after all you've gone through. It's too late for crying now."

She nodded vigorously at him and didn't speak, but nudged him lightly.

They walked out together, and hundreds of eyes watched them come.

An officer came toward them. He was amazingly clean and freshly shaven. At least he looked that way in the growing light.

"Who are you?"

"I'm Jess Swindin, train scout for Jacob Harter of Clybourne. This is Miss Elizabeth Mellon, daughter of the wagon-maker at Clybourne. We were both trying to get to Camp Lincoln for help when some white renegades in soldiers' uniforms caught us."

"In Army uniforms?" the officer said, blinking at them both.

"Yes, from Fort Ten-Mile."

"How did they get them from Ten-Mile? Must have killed a sentry or two."

141

Jess shook his head gravely. "Afraid it's worse than that. Fort Ten-Mile was wiped out. The garrison; women, children, and all. After that the hostiles struck at Clybourne, but the relief column for Ten-Mile came back in time to rout the Indians."

The silence was suddenly deeper. For a long time the officer just looked from Elizabeth to Jess; then he said, "Have either of you been to Ten-Mile to verify this?"

"I have," Jess said. "I scouted for the Clybourne wagon train. We buried as many as we could before we hurried back to Clybourne."

"And there were no survivors? You quite sure of that?"

"I'm as sure as I am that we're standing here."

Jess was fretting. He sympathized with the officer's shocked condition but didn't condone it. A glance beyond at the sea of grey faces and still eyes told him the other troopers had heard him plainly enough.

"I crippled that renegade you have there when we ran for it. There are two more up ahead running for an Indian village and one behind us somewhere—unless you found him. These four white men led the Indians, or at least planned their strategy for them."

The officer shook himself like a dog coming out of the water. He half-turned and threw up a thick arm. In a toneless voice he said, "There's a dead white man we found on the trail back of you. He'd been slashed from ear to ear."

Stunned, Jess stared at the corpse lashed over a pack mule. He walked toward it, squatted and looked up at the mottled face. "That's one of them. That's the one they called Starr." He pushed himself upright and gazed at Elizabeth. She was dry-eyed now and pale. "There *were* Indians behind us, then." He took two steps away

142

from the burdened mule, then stopped. "No, no—I know what it was. Elizabeth, remember when Goddard came back, he was out of breath?" He could see instantly that she had guessed it too. There had been bad blood between Starr and Goddard. "He went far out and around us, came up behind Starr and cut his throat, then ran like the devil to get ahead of us again."

Elizabeth nodded gently at him but still wouldn't trust herself to speak.

The officer dropped his arm and ignored the corpse. "Where did the others go?"

"Up ahead, eastward. They said there's an Indian encampment up there. Some of the Sioux and Cheyennes who were in on the Ten-Mile massacre and the attack on Clybourne. Iron Shirt's village."

"Iron Shirt," the officer breathed. Without another wasted moment he made a slashing gesture with a fisted arm. "Mount the troops. Swindin, you ride with me. Reilly, detach twenty men to take Miss Mellon to the rear and guard her. Lieutenant Swanson—move out!"

The daylight was pleasant only because the sun hadn't quite made it over the top of the sawtoothed mountains yet. Jess heard someone say "Wait," and turned to look. It was Elizabeth holding up her escort while she pulled in close beside him. Looking up into his face, she asked, "Why can't we go the rest of the way together?"

"There may be fighting."

"Then come back with me. You've done your share. Let the soldiers do it."

He smiled at her fondly. "They'll have to; I'm too tired right now. No; go on back, Liz, and—"

He tapered off lamely. He was looking down into her face in the new light, seeing her clearly for the first time

143

after so many harrowing hours. She was tired, her cheeks were sunken, and there were blue circles under her eyes. She was strangely beautiful.

She prompted him. "Yes?"

"Be careful," he said, drawing in a big breath as his horse began to move along with the other horses. "Take care of yourself; I want you to."

The thick-armed, broad-shouldered commanding officer said something impatiently. Jess didn't hear the words, only the tone. He tightened his knees and caught up.

"Good thing we brought extra animals."

Jess' eyes were fixed on the distance ahead. "Extra ammunition too, I hope," he said with an effort, forcing his mind from gentler things.

The officer looked thoughtfully bleak. "Enough, I think. How many Indians are up here, do you know?"

"No, but I think it's a pretty big village. The way the renegades talked, they must be lying around waiting for their messengers to bring back other tribesmen. The massacre'll incite every strong-heart buck in the Territory."

"I suppose," the officer said; then he was silent for a while. "You were at Ten-Mile?"

"Yes."

"Tell me about it."

Jess did, reciting every detail he recalled. While he spoke his eyes were on the two Indian scouts far ahead, ranging the land like experienced hunting dogs, their upper bodies naked, their legs and feet encased in buckskin. Both had notched feathers in their hair and, except that their backs were to the blue column, could have been hostiles.

He was watching them when they both stopped, said something to one another and stared straight

144

ahead, rigid, on their horses. One made a quick, nervous hand gesture, putting his palms together, fingers straight and outward, then drawing his hands apart simultaneously.

"Big." Then, rapidly moving his hands together with all but the first fingers closed, he crossed the fingers so that they leaned into one another. "Village."

"They see the village and it's a big one."

Grim, pained eyes regarded Jess briefly. "You understand that sign-talk—that *wibluta?*"

"Yes."

A young officer with fiery red hair and a waxed mustache trotted back. The commander twisted, cast a long look down his column, then settled forward in the saddle again. "Send out skirmishers, Eric. Put them under Flannery. Form up two attacking ranks. Sabers and pistols. Watch for my signal."

It was all very coolly done. Jess felt left out in a way. The columns broke up, converged again and became separate striking forces. He looked far back but saw no trace of Elizabeth. He knew about where she was. Then he kicked out his Army horse and went ahead with the skirmishers.

There was a lift and fall to the prairie that hid the Indian village. He breasted it when the soldiers did, reined up and sat there.

If Ten-Mile had been a massacre, this was a miracle. The Sioux hadn't had more than a half-hour's warning of their approach; yet, facing them in a long, barbaric line of vivid splendor, was the Indian army.

There were two solid ranks of them that stretched all along the rise in the prairie, facing the skirmishers. There wasn't a sound coming from them. A little lost breeze stirred their feathers and otter-tail spangles. Color was

145

everywhere—on the warriors, on the horses, even on the hide lodges far down the land behind them.

Jess heard the sounds in the village where the women were striking the camp. Lodges were coming down, travois were being loaded, children cried out occasionally and dogs barked. A shrill yelp now and then indicated some squaw had kicked a dog out of her way. Strangely, there were no wails.

The scene was a primitive one. He brought his glance back to the warriors. Several older men with war bonnets were riding up and down before their fighting bucks as unconcerned, as scornful and deliberately contemptuous as they could be. He heard a ripple of admiration go down the line of mounted skirmishers. A nervous soldier next to him swore mildly and said, "Sure a lot of 'em."

"There'll be more after today," Jess said, "and if you don't whip them they'll have another victory to celebrate. A couple more victories like Ten-Mile, and you won't lick them for ten years."

The soldier swung his head anxiously and watched the main column galloping toward them. Without looking back at the Indians again, he said, "We got no edge."

Jess said nothing. He'd noticed that too. It would be an even fight; no odds, no concessions. He drew in a rattling, deep breath.

CHAPTER IX

THERE HAD BEEN NO NEED FOR THE SKIRMISHERS, BUT IT was a regulation requirement and therefore had become a habit to throw them out ahead of the main column.

Now, atop the little rib of land, they sat there like

statues, facing the big force of Indians whose ranks curved back and inward a little, protecting their village. With no waste effort and a minimum of confusion the camp was being broken up speedily.

The Army came at an unhurried trot. Steady and experienced, no orders rippled through the quiet, broken only by insignificant sounds. If there was any emotion on the bronzed faces it was grim vengeance, not fright nor anxiety.

Then they too were riding up the hill and the skirmishers' ranks were filled to overflowing with the might of the Camp Lincoln garrison. They didn't stop or even pause, but scooped up the skirmishers, as if it had all been rehearsed, and swept on over the swell and down the other side, still at the trot.

Jess rode with them, Mike's carbine clutched sweatily in his right fist, reins in his left. Little triangular guidons fluttered. Among the blues they were the only splash of color. Orange, red, purple, slashed with black outlines of curved sabres, crossed against the contrasting backgrounds.

Then the Indians let out an anticipatory yell and the spell was broken. Jess saw the way the veterans lifted themselves a little in the saddle, leaned forward a trifle, unconsciously bracing against the shock of meeting the Indian line.

A spanking, short blast on a bugle, some indistinct orders throated in a snarling way, drifted above the hoof-thunder. Jess thought: This is it! He knew that call just as he knew the high-pitched scream of a Sioux war-leader.

"HOKA HAY!" (Charge!!)

Then the silence was irretrievably shattered. The Indians raised the yell. It was blood-curdling and

147

deafening. Without the restraint of the soldier ranks, they booted out their war-horses. The best animals carried their riders far ahead of the slower beasts. War bonnets with long trailers whipped under the sparkling sun. Lances with dyed scalp-locks were lowered and leveled and over a thousand painted faces were contorted until neck muscles strained beneath dusky hides. The war-cry of the Dakota Nation!

Jess raised up a little too, when the shock came. The ranks struck with stunning, jarring force. For a fraction of a second there was silence; then the guns began to rattle and roar. The fight was on.

He shot a wild look at the soldiers around him. For the most part they fought in silence, slit-lipped, slashing their big sabres in graceful arcs or firing their long-barreled Dragoon pistols with fast, steady accuracy. The line would hold, then break through the frenzied warriors. These were all veterans.

After that one short look Jess was occupied. It was a kaleidoscope of action, counter-action, noise, bedlam, confusion, wild, straining faces and exploding weapons. He fought instinctively without seeking a target, for none was stationary enough to seek. When he fired the carbine it was because an Indian careened across his path and appeared before him where no Indian had been seconds before. If he killed a man or ten men, he never knew it. All he was certain of was that, after the initial shock, the first wild joining, his carbine was empty.

He dropped it and drew his pistol. He knew when he fired it by the kick against his palm and thumb-pad, but he couldn't distinguish one gun's roar among the thousand other guns also exploding.

Then they were through the Indians and riding in a rolling gallop toward the village. The officers shouted then. The ranks closed up where gaps were; swung into a semblance of orderliness. From this, Jess took heart anew.

The Indians came in behind them shrieking demons, their firepower still devastating, their accuracy negligible. Several bands of warriors streaked around the ends of the soldiers' ranks and swung wide to come around facing the blues, in front of the panicked village. It was a valorous gesture but useless. The Army didn't even waver. When it was close enough gunfire erupted along the front line. Dirty grey smoke drifted rearward. The die-hard warriors had done just that, almost to a man.

Then they were in among the scurrying, screeching squaws who fought wildly with whatever was at hand— broken lodge-poles, sticks snatched up hastily from the still smoldering breakfast fires. Bows were handled clumsily. A few had long cavalry sabres they swung like scythes.

There was no mercy in that blue line. No face registered pity, even. Jess saw two squaws drag a man off his horse. One had a wicked-looking knife upraised when several troopers flashed past, sitting lightly sideways, pistols raised. He looked away quickly.

The fight lasted a full two hours before the Indians began to give way a little. In possession of the village, the Army had cover at last. Amid the jumble of horses shot dead in their travois lashings, the jumble and tangle of struck tepees, the multitude of personal possessions scattered indiscriminately by dogs, horses, people, the soldiers could lie, or kneel, and fire. The plunging back of a horse was no place even to hope for accuracy.

Jess watched the Sioux and Cheyennes retreat stubbornly. He saw the way a lot of the fighting

149

warriors wouldn't yield an inch of ground and were riddled, still screaming defiance and shaking their empty guns.

A man he saw, wearing a war bonnet with dual trailers of eagle feathers, was walking—not running—away from his downed horse. The beast threshed and the big Indian walked away, deliberately presenting his back to the soldiers. Jess held his fire, almost held his breath. The first heat of his blood had passed. He let his pistol sag where he knelt, just watching.

The Sioux leader of some kind winced once, missed a step but went on without walking a bit faster or turning to face his enemies. Then he stumbled, sagged, waited a moment, got his balance and went on again. Jess stood up, fascinated.

The big buck went down, was prone for a moment, with dust-banners being kicked up all around him by the soldiers' fire. Then, unbelievably, he pushed himself upright, took a tentative step, another, another . . .

Someone was yelling like a wild man, howling encouragement to the Indian.

The Indian went down again. That time he rolled over onto his back and Jess could see the scarlet that smeared his naked chest and belly. Another scream of admiration, of encouragement trickled off as two warriors leaped off their horses, ran to the downed man, lifted him between them, turned and dragged him away, his back still to the soldiers.

Jess made a choking sound. He hadn't recognized the yelling voice as his own, but a sergeant nearby had seen him yelling encouragement. He stood up, spat, looked askew at Jess and shook his head.

"I don't blame you. You can hate 'em—but they got guts."

Everything that happened after that was anticlimax. The fight was over except for sniping and skirmishing. The Army had the village, or what remained of it. They had the buffalo bladders of *wasna,* the Sioux K-ration made of dried meat and condiments. They had the battlefield and had driven off the attackers who attempted to resecure the village. They also had the lowest casualty rate, from the looks of the blood-slippery area. So they had victory.

But the Indians weren't through. They fought on in small parties, as individuals, in pairs and as fanatics. More than once a single warrior, freshly painted, singing his death-chant at the top of his lungs, charged the entire Army alone. It was like murder to watch. There was no other way though. The Army had special squads, rarely more than four sharpshooters, who dispatched these heroic tribesmen. No one had stomach for the job, but it had to be done.

Jess' reaction was setting in now. He sought the creek behind the wreckage of the village and stripped off his grimy shirt, listlessly bathed the upper part of his body and felt the tingling coldness of the water. Lying down full length under the willows there, he felt the revival of his energy. He was still there when the soldiers began to lead their horses over to water, and wash out the hurts of the wounded animals. There was very little said among the troopers and none of them spoke to Jess at all.

He lay there for over an hour with the occasional, distant pop of a pistol, or carbine or rifle, emphasizing the silence.

"Jess?"

He lifted his head. "Hello, Elizabeth."

"They told me you were down here. Are you hurt?"

He laid his head back down and looked up through

the dappling leaf shadows at the brassy, bleached out sky. "No, not hurt, but tired and plumb tuckered out, Elizabeth. I feel whipped and worn out and a little sick inside, but not wounded."

She came closer, sat down beside him facing the creek, drew her feet under her and gazed down at his face. The dark beard-stubble made him look older. The tiredness, the dry-eyed expression, the blank, empty, exhausted, almost stupid look cut her under the heart like a knife.

"It's all over now, Jess."

He didn't speak or move or act as if he knew or cared that she was there.

"We had to come this far—go through all that—to have Clybourne made safe."

"Clybourne," he said softly, "doesn't even know it."

"No, that's what I mean. Way out here in Indian country we did it. You and I."

He propped his head up on one powerful arm and looked at her with a twinkle of the old humor showing. "Well, the Army did a little of it, Elizabeth. I think we ought to give them at least a nod of thanks."

She smiled wistfully down at him. "You feel better now, don't you? Would you like me to soak my handkerchief in the water and wash your face?"

"Is it very dirty? I washed it a little while ago."

"It's pretty dirty," she said, moving toward the water.

He watched her. Her skirt was dusty-looking. There were two torn places in it. She bent low at the creek. All he could see was her profile. Her strong, sturdy arms were bare to the elbows in the water. He thought it remarkable that she could look so pretty after all she'd been through.

"Lie back down. There, does that feel better?"

He didn't answer. Her face, above him, was like a drug. Her lashes had a lilting, upward curve to them. Her mouth, full-lipped, was miraculously unchanged and cool-looking. Unconsciously he ran the tip of his tongue over his own cracked lips and felt the fever in them.

She rocked back on her haunches and smiled at him. "You know, Jess, you're a handsome man. Even with those prickly whiskers, you're a handsome man." Her smile died slowly, and for a moment she didn't say anything. Then she shrugged, shifted her glance away from his watching eyes, looked a little on the defensive and said, with a hint of defiance in her tone, "I've already said things to you I shouldn't have, so I can't say them again very well." For a second confusion showed in her glance. "Well, don't just lie there; say something. Tell me you're not interested. Tell me to be still—anything."

He started to speak, but his voice betrayed him with a croaking sound. He cleared his throat and started again. That time it was all right.

"Liz, you're beautiful and I'm very much in love with you."

"You've never said it before."

He looked dumbfounded. He started to say something, pushed himself upright and rolled his eyes in a helpless way. "Maybe I was just too scairt to say it."

"Afraid of me?" she asked innocently.

"Well, it wasn't the Indians, I can promise you that."

"Jess?"

"Yes."

"Tell me you love me in *wibluta*. That hand-talking fascinates me."

Obediently he made a fist of his right hand with the

153

thumb sticking out. He turned the pointed thumb inward and touched his chest with it. "That means I, or me."

Next he crossed his arms at the wrists, fingers fisted and right arm in, against his body; then he brought both crossed arms in against his chest and repeated the movement. "That means love. It also means fondness. Sort of like holding someone against your heart."

He pointed his right hand at Elizabeth exactly as a white person points, index finger extended. "You."

She glanced quickly away from him, then back again. "It's poetic, isn't it? The way they say love, for instance. It's very beautiful, Jess."

"I'll teach it to you, if you'd like."

"I'd like that."

A man's solid footfalls interrupted them. The sweat-drenched commanding officer loomed up and looked with a puzzled expression at them. He nodded to Elizabeth and swung his glance to Jess.

"Are you all right? I saw you motioning toward your chest a moment ago as I was coming through the willows. Aren't wounded, are you?"

Jess smiled for the first time in days. "No, I'm just fine." He shot Elizabeth an amused glance.

The officer nodded. "Fine, I'm glad you aren't hurt. We've got two white men up here we'd like you to identify for us if you can. They say they're traders, but I doubt that."

"Be glad to," Jess said. "Be right up. By the way, are you going on to Clybourne when you're finished here?"

"Yes, I think we'd better pull out as soon as we're through burning the village, before the moon comes up and the daylight's gone."

"Good."

They watched the burly officer walk back up toward

154

the village; then Elizabeth laughed in a soft, musical way. "Sign-language has an advantage over spoken languages, hasn't it? He didn't understand what you told me. If he had we'd both have been embarrassed to death."

Jess grabbed up his shirt and stood up. He felt thoroughly recovered. Without speaking, he held out his free hand. She took it, and he pulled her to her feet. Then, almost as though they had rehearsed it, he pulled her still farther. She went up against him and clung there. His cracked, sore mouth sought hers. It was miraculously cool and soft, like velvet.

We hope that you enjoyed reading this Sagebrush Large Print Western. If you would like to read more Sagebrush titles, ask your librarian or contact the Publishers:

United States and Canada

Thomas T. Beeler, *Publisher*
Post Office Box 659
Hampton Falls, New Hampshire 03844-0659
(800) 818-7574

United Kingdom, Eire, and the Republic of South Africa

Isis Publishing Ltd
7 Centremead
Osney Mead
Oxford OX2 0ES England
(01865) 250333

Australia and New Zealand

Bolinda Publishing Pty. Ltd.
17 Mohr Street
Tullamarine, 3043, Victoria, Australia
(016103) 9338 0666